Camping with Strangers

Camping with Strangers

STORIES

Sarah Nawrocki

Boaz Publishing Company | Albany, California

Distributed by Publishers Group West

Address all inquiries to Boaz Publishing Company,
Post Office Box 6582, Albany, CA 94706 (510) 525-9459

Designed by April Leidig-Higgins
Set in Electra by Eric M. Brooks
Printed in the United States of America

This is a work of fiction. Names, places, characters,
and incidents either are the products of the author's
imagination or are used fictitiously, and any resemblance
to events, locales, or actual persons, living or dead,
is entirely coincidental.

Library of Congress Cataloging-in-Publication Data
Nawrocki, Sarah.   Camping with strangers: stories /
Sarah Nawrocki.   p. cm.   Contents: Louise and Al get
married—Locusts—Dogs—Pampas grass day—Pressure—
Boys—Hovercraft—Farmer boy—Star seed—Camping
with strangers. ISBN 0-9651879-9-3   1. United States—
Social life and customs—20th century—Fiction.   I. Title.
PS3564.A8934C3   1999   813'.54—dc21   99-17582   CIP

Special thanks to Judy Bloch, Marjorie Fowler,
Tom Southern, Denise Stallcup, and
Elizabeth Vahlsing.

Some of these stories first appeared in the following
magazines: "Boys" in Shenandoah; "Camping with
Strangers" in the American Literary Review; "Pampas
Grass Day" in the South Dakota Review; "Locusts"
in the Artful Dodge; and "Star Seed" in the
Pikeville Review.

For Brian

Contents

Camping with Strangers

Louise and Al Get Married

The man she is going to marry has a mole on the left side of his face and a worried expression when he thinks no one is looking. The worry reminds her of responsibility. He's as conscientious as they come, she can tell, even though he is also carefree and sometimes funny. In the years that follow, she will discover she has made a mistake. Her husband will fear freeways and train stations, spring and exotic foods, bright colors, the possibility of travel. There is safety in the home and no place else, he'll say. She'll be restless and impatient, full of revelations and no direction all at once, impulsive, unimpressed by caution. But by then they'll be used to it, the way people who are invested in a bad idea hold it up to the light, trying hard to see its worth.

Now their future stretches out before them, road into the sunset, happily ever after, a greeting card of unfocused flowers and pink ribbons.

"Al," Louise says, "can you hand me an orange? I'm hungry."

And Al does it. He brings her an orange from the fridge, shines it on his shirt, hands her a paper napkin and a knife to make the peeling easier. That is how much he loves her.

"There you go," he says, and sits down beside her. The couch squeaks with his weight, which isn't very much—he's such a skinny guy. When they are married and safe, money in the bank and brand new everything, they might get a better couch, sturdy springs, tasteful upholstery. They'll leave that old hide-a-bed from Louise's grandmother by the dumpster.

Louise peels the orange. Juice runs down her hands to her wrists. She chews on the rind and sighs, and the smell of citrus fills the air.

"Use the napkin," Al says. He hates a mess.

"Sorry." Louise takes the napkin and wipes her hands. Bits of blue paper stick to her fingers.

Louise and Al are trying to figure out how to tell their parents the big news, that they're going to be joined at the hip—not an operation, but almost as serious. They want to do it right, because all the wedding books they've seen at the library emphasize the proper over everything else. No matter that the groom may be blind and the church a maze; he should walk down the aisle by himself. The guests should sit at tables in the places bearing their name cards, regardless of whether they want to organize themselves differently. The bride should behave as though this is the biggest day of her life, even if she swears surviving a terrible car accident years ago meant more in the grand scheme of things. None of the books mention how big a day it's supposed to be for the groom; Louise and Al suspect he's supposed to take it all in stride.

"We could call our parents," Al says.

Louise hands him an orange section. "Yes, we could. Or we could write them."

"Write? They live across town. What's the point of that?" Al waves the orange around when he talks. Verbal hands, just like his father. A piece of pulp lands on Louise's arm, cold and a little slimy.

"Careful, there," she says. "Watch it with that orange."

He pops it in his mouth and chews. "Thowy," he says, his mouth full. He blots the spot on her arm with a piece of the shredded napkin.

"I just think that would make it real for them. A letter, I mean. No doubt about it with a letter."

"I don't see why."

"They can refer to it over and over again, for proof," Louise says. "In case they're having a hard time coming to terms with it."

"Keep the enclosed copy for your records. Something like that?"

Louise nods and rubs her fingers along her teeth. An awful habit. Never touch your ears or teeth, rub your eyes or nose, scratch your face in public. Unprofessional, unsightly. Rules to live by. Her mother recited them in her low voice, like telling a secret. But

Louise loves to feel her teeth, so solid, the hardest part of her. She'll have to quit before the wedding.

She can see from Al's face, his brow all wrinkled, that he still doesn't like the letter idea. His parents will be baffled. He hasn't mailed them anything since college, and that was just the occasional card. They won't know what to make of it. As if he were running away, note on the kitchen table. Gone off to live with Louise. Don't know when I'll be back. Same thing, really. Louise knows this: she is the one who will take him from them, grown man in a little basket, bundled up in a blue blanket, his head peeking over the edge.

Al looks at her and smiles. He's made up his mind. "Better phone them instead," he says. "Why don't I call right now?"

Louise sinks back into the couch. She watches Al dial, his long fingers precise, delicate, like a surgeon's or a musician's. Piano hands, except he doesn't play anything, not counting the kazoo. The room is still and quiet, heavy with their anticipation.

Louise wanted to be a drummer in a rock band when she was in sixth grade. It was the first year the kids could take lessons at school, marching band, jazz band, concerts with the junior high choir, and she told her parents all they needed to do was sign the slip giving permission.

Her father folded his arms across his chest and leaned back in his chair. "Why do you need to do that?" he said. "Girls don't play drums."

Her mother looked down at her lap, inspecting a piece of food stuck to her skirt.

"How about a nice horn?" he said. "Clarinet? Flute?"

"Those are wind instruments," Louise said. "Forget it."

Her father reached across the table and pointed to the bowl next to her. "Pass the peas, sweets," he said, and she did. That was the end of that.

Then Louise thought she might be a veterinarian, but she couldn't stand the thought of doing all those operations, giving dire diagnoses to dogs and cats who didn't know about cars, roads, looking both ways. She just wanted to pet them and tell them ridiculous things, the way she does now to Franklin and Moose, the cats she and Al

3

found wandering in the parking lot outside the Bestway. Aren't you fierce, and Scooberdoodle, and Franklin the Great, names and whole sentences she says when no one is around. The cats look at her and blink, go back to licking their paws or sleeping.

Those are the only two professions she can think of: vet or drummer. Everything else she can take or leave. Data entry seems about the same as answering the phone at a construction company, which is what she's doing now. Al says her ambition will arrive one day when she isn't looking, the way lovers appear from nowhere in romance novels, but Louise isn't so sure. She'll still be saying "drummer or vet" when she's eighty, brittle bones and spidery hands. It's never too late, after all.

———————

Al talks to his parents in the slow voice he uses with his elementary students. "Yes, that's right," he's saying. "Engaged, yes."

Louise strains to hear what they're saying on the other end. She imagines them in the living room of their yellow house, cocked back in their easy chairs, watching golf on TV. The little white ball rolling to the hole or missing it completely, the hushed clapping, people murmuring under their breath, as if in a dream.

"No, not yet," Al says, glancing at her. "We don't have a date yet. But you'll be the first to know when we do."

Louise smiles at him and rolls her eyes. They should have known this would be the first question; if you're getting married, you're supposed to choose a day. All the books say that. They'll never get away with posting it somewhere in the future, vast, indefinite. A letter would have been better, all the questions answered in Al's perfect handwriting, every word square and determined. "We're working on the date now. More to come"—phrases like that.

"Yes," Al is saying. "Mmm hmm. Of course, Mom. We—" He hands the phone to Louise. "She wants to talk to you."

"Bad?" she mouths, because she doesn't want Al's mom to hear. She's a little afraid of his parents, their hospital-clean house, no dust motes hanging in the air. Louise has come to think of dust as friendly, benevolent, proof of life or at least of a lack of cleaning agents.

Al shakes his head and frowns. "Just take the phone," he whispers, and points to the handset, which she's cradling in her lap.

4

"Hello," she says.

"Louise. Our new daughter." Al's mother's voice is shrill, excited.

"Yes, that's me. It's something, all right."

"What are you going to wear?"

"You mean to the wedding?"

"Yes, what else? Back when we got married, you built the entire wedding around the dress. The dress is the centerpiece, and of course, so is the bride inside."

Louise doesn't know. She imagines herself in a long puffy dress, train behind her like a tail, her head tiny, almost invisible. The bride inside. "Something white," she says.

Al's mother laughs. "Well, that's a relief. White is good."

They talk some more, about how much time, really, is needed to plan these events, the virtue of organization skills, how to make lists and be vigilant about revising them. Louise looks over at Al, who's lying on the floor with Franklin on his stomach. He grimaces and shrugs, and Franklin slides to the floor, too sleepy to right himself.

"Al is the best boy in the world," his mother is saying now, "and I'm certain he's found the best girl."

Louise snorts. Her horse laugh, Al calls it. She'll have to stop doing that before the wedding, too. She thinks his mom might be serious, but what should she say? "Thank you," she finally manages.

"You're welcome, dear."

She gives the phone to Al and scoops up Franklin. He likes to be held, shoulder level, in front of the windows. He can see so much from that height, Louise thinks. He looks past the hedge to the lawn, and his nose twitches, anxious. He sees something, maybe a bird or a squirrel foraging for pecans. "Fierce one," she whispers, and rubs her face in his fur. She can hear Al talking to his father now, going over the same things again, patient, calm, the perfect boy.

The way they got engaged was like this. They were doing their weekly shopping at the Bestway. Al had the list and two or three coupons, and Louise pushed the cart along, pulling cereal and tortillas, skim milk, tomato sauce off the shelves. They might have burgers for supper, but maybe not; it depended on how they felt when they got to the beef section. Sometimes the wormy, brainy texture of the meat disgusted them, and other times it was just a bunch of ground meat to fry up into patties, that's all.

In the produce section, there was a brand new shipment of exotic fruits, kumquats and pomegranates, kiwis, mangoes, and even plantains. Someone had arranged them in small mounds, little pyramids of fruit with a cardboard sign sticking out of the top giving the name, origin, and serving suggestions.

"Look at all that," Louise said. "All those foods."

"Yeah," Al said. "Isn't there a myth about pomegranates?"

"I don't know, but we should try one. I ate one years ago in elementary school."

"Yeah, probably to go along with the myth you were studying. The one we don't remember."

Louise picked up two pomegranates and put them in the cart. They felt firm, contained, in her hands. She stared at the kumquats, tiny and brilliant, a cross between an egg and an orange.

"Perfect things," she said, and tossed two of them in the air. She could juggle them if she wanted to. An old man called The General, who lived across the alley from the house she'd grown up in, had a kumquat tree, and the fruits would fall at some point, covering the alley and finally rotting. It never occurred to her to eat them.

"Go ahead and get some of those, too," Al said. He was smiling, the gap between his teeth showing, a souvenir from the time he went down the slide face first in fifth grade. "They're a cool shape. I can't imagine how to peel one, but it says right here on the sign that it's safe to eat the peel. Apparently it's very thin."

"Hmm," Louise said. She grabbed a handful of kumquats and started to put them in a plastic bag. But they were so handsome, proof of something, the vastness of the world brought right to her doorstep. She held them in her hand, peered closely. A peel you could eat. A fruit that was like an orange, but not the same. Greatness to be found in one's neighborhood grocery store. Later, she would realize how corny it was. But real, too, and all of a sudden she turned to Al, who was selecting a bunch of bananas in the next aisle.

"Hey," she said, "Al."

He looked up, and there was his sweet face, full of absent worry, the way it was when he was considering nothing in particular. She tried to think of a way to explain about the kumquats, about all the choices in the world, things they couldn't even see or know about. They were meant to eat kumquats and wander together; she was sure of it.

A woman bumped her arm, reaching past her to get some of the tiny fruits. Her hands were thick, pale, and she tossed the kumquats into her bag like stones. Her face was stern. She seemed to be in a hurry.

Louise moved out of her way.

"What?" Al said.

"Uh—marry me," she said. She looked around, surprised. She hadn't planned it. The woman next to her stared, clutching her bag of fruit to her chest.

"Huh? Carry the kumquats?" Al said. He hadn't heard. "Just put them in the cart. It's right behind you."

Louise looked at the shopping cart, full of their bread and milk, everything they needed. She felt slow, dull.

"No."

Louise whirled around. It was the woman next to her. She was talking to Al, her voice loud, authoritative. Al tilted his head to one side, listening hard, confused maybe.

"No, that's not what she said. She said 'Marry me,' not 'Carry these.'" The woman spoke precisely, especially "marry me," as if Al were not a native speaker of English.

"Oh," Al said. "Okay." He nodded, smiled, kept on nodding. "Okay," he said again. "Okay, Louise, I do. I mean, I will."

The woman walked toward the onions and potatoes at the end of the row, her short legs stiff and heavy. She didn't say anything else.

Louise looked down and saw that she was holding a bag of fruit, the kumquats still there. She'd forgotten about them. Pictures of her life with Al filled her head: their cats, their witty children, their gray hair and bony limbs, even their eventual deaths.

"Good," she said. "It's a deal." She wheeled the cart over to where Al was standing, nearly knocking down two boys in front of the pistachio bin on the way. She couldn't get over it—one minute shopping, the next engaged.

She put out her hand to shake on it, and Al bent to kiss her. In the evening, she and Al would sit on the front steps of their apartment,

7

eating the kumquats and swatting at mosquitoes, watching the neighborhood kids ride by on their bicycles.

The customers at the construction company say Louise has the perfect phone voice. You're always ready to help, one said. You listen to me just like my mother used to, another told her. And, I feel I've known you all my life. Just from her voice one man said that. Louise isn't sure what to make of it. True, she likes the idea of being good at her job—because not everyone can answer the phone all day long in a nice voice. But reminding someone of their long-lost mother? It makes her nervous. Nothing more than a bunch of invisible sound waves squeezing their way through the telephone lines from her mouth right into some stranger's ear.

"B and J Construction, may I help you," she says, all day long. "No sir, he's not in the office. Would you like to leave a message?" Hard to find anyone you know buried in that. On bad days, when too many customers rhapsodize about her voice, she grows cranky and short. "B and J, hold please," she says, and when she picks up the line again, the customers say, "Where's Louise? Is she out sick today?" Really, it's only three or four of them, but they seem to call more than average.

One of the best things about Al is that he's never noticed her voice, one way or the other. He can see deeper; he knows she isn't just a noise at the other end of the phone.

"What do you think of my voice?" she said one day, just to be sure. They were at the McDonald's drive-thru, and the intercom hissed with static while a man with a cold, his words unclear, took their order.

Al was counting the bills in his wallet, whispering the numbers to himself. "Your voice," he said, "your voice is—seven, eight, nine— It's fine."

"But do you think it's especially good or bad?" Louise hated to dig for details, but it was important.

Al looked at her and raised his eyebrows, suspicious. "I like it," he said. "It's very nice."

The clerk told them to drive to the window around the corner to pick up their food.

"Hold these," Al said, and handed her a few dollars.

Louise didn't see how she could bring it up again. She sighed and leaned back in her seat. The car smelled of hot vinyl and gasoline, and the sun shone in on her side. She could see the dust covering the dashboard and floating in the air, and she basked in the warmth of her ordinariness.

———

Al hangs up the phone. "It's a mistake," he says. He shakes his head and kicks his sneakers off one at a time. They land against the wall with a soft thud. Moose runs over and scratches her paws on the gray shiny material of the shoes, as if she's digging for treasure.

Louise feels cold. A mistake. That sounds bad. She imagines Al hunched over his fourth graders' papers, red pencil poised to circle a spelling error. It could be a little mistake. "What do you mean?" she says, and forces herself to keep flipping through the magazine she's been reading.

"We should have told them in person," Al says. "Should have made them dinner, announced it just as they were taking a big bite of some fancy dessert, maybe that chocolate cake you make with the raspberry sauce."

"We decided on calling," she says. "You wanted to call."

"Yes, but only because a visit hadn't occurred to me."

"They live twenty minutes away, at least."

"Exactly," Al says. "Just across town." He sits on the floor and stretches his legs out in front of him, wiggles his feet from side to side. Louise can tell he hasn't changed his socks in a day or two; a sour, stale odor rises from them.

"Al, your feet really do stink," she says, even though she knows it's rude. She turns her head away to avoid the smell.

"Laundry. It's the next thing on my list."

They're both quiet for a moment, watching Al wiggle his toes inside his socks. Then Al says, "Crap," which is his favorite swear word.

"It's fine," she says, "fine. I don't think they'll notice anyway."

But Al just shakes his head. "My dad already did." He lowers his chin so his neck thickens, and deepens his voice—his imitation of his father. "'How come you didn't drive on over, son? We could've

9

broke out the champagne from New Year's and taken you out. Your mother would have liked that.'"

Louise folds her arms across her chest. "Your mom didn't seem to mind."

"I'm just saying, that's what he said."

Louise imagines the possibilities: They rush over there now, a store-bought frozen cake thawing in their arms, and shout, "Surprise!" They call back and cancel, say it was all a mistake, and then drive over and take his parents to Red Lobster, which is Al's father's favorite restaurant, and tell them again. They do nothing and go to her parents' house instead, knowing all the while that Louise's mother is probably taking a nap—her favorite pastime—and her father is mowing the lawn outside her bedroom window—his favorite pastime—and neither will be pleased to see Al and Louise unannounced.

None of these ideas is good. "We can't go back now," she says. "There's no way to undo it. We're stuck."

"Stuck like a bug on the wall." Al snaps his fingers, and Moose chirrups and races over to him.

Louise frowns. She's never heard him say that. "Reduced to cliches," she says. "Don't you mean 'bump on a log'?"

"Reduced, all right. That is the right word. Because I know we're going to hear about this mistake until we die."

No, she thinks, until his parents die. "Possibly," she says. "But now we have to call my parents. Because your parents will be even madder if they find out we told my parents in person."

"I didn't say they were mad."

"What, then?"

"They're just disappointed, that's all."

"Disappointed, mad, what's the difference?"

"Mad is stronger."

Louise sighs and shrugs. Al is getting picky, which is how their worst fights usually start. "Whatever," she says, and rattles the pages of her magazine, the way her father used to shake the newspaper when she and her mother talked too much at breakfast.

Louise's parents are still married, although who can say why? They despise each other quietly, careful not to let it rise to the surface too often. They staked out opposite sides of the house years ago. Her father has claimed the backyard for his gardening while her mother tends the pots of flowers near the front door. Her father gets the garage, and her mother has the study, the living room, and the bedroom. Louise is pretty sure her father sleeps on the couch in the TV room, his arms folded across his chest, his legs crossed, as if he is watching television in his sleep.

Each tells Louise secrets about the other: Your mother takes naps all the time, but don't tell her I said so. Your father drinks wine for breakfast with his eggs. He stays up until four a.m. watching bad cable shows. But I know you won't make a big deal out of it. She never loved me. He never loved us. It gets so Louise can't stay more than a few hours at a time. Her parents steal her momentum. After a visit, she stares at the walls of the apartment for hours, as if the cracks and spackling hold hidden answers only she will find.

Louise sighs and slaps the magazine closed. Outside, the light is gray and dull, early evening. The November sky hovers thick overhead. In a few weeks, they'll be huddled in blankets, trying to stay warm in the draft, their apartment walls too thin against the wind.

"We should call my parents now," Louise says. "What if your parents get to them first? They'll be confused." She imagines Al's mother talking to her mom, telling her all about how the wedding should be centered on the dress. Her mother would pause a long time and then say "What?" in that slow, outraged way of hers.

"Right now?"

"We can't let too much time pass." Louise reaches for the phone. It feels cold and heavy in her hands. "Maybe they won't be home," she mumbles.

"Maybe."

The phone rings and rings. Louise counts. After the fifth ring, she begins to feel hopeful. They might be out. When she was young and first learning to use the phone, her mother said to let it ring five times, and if no one answered, it was probably a good idea to hang up. Maybe she'd been calling relatives or the girl next door and letting the phone ring for minutes. Or maybe she'd been hanging up too soon, before the lines even had a chance to connect. And now look at her, juggling ten lines at once, all day every day, the picture of calm stuck at a desk.

When her father picks up the phone, on the ninth ring, Louise has forgotten why she's calling. "Hello," he says, and his voice is tired, a little irritated.

"Hey," she says, "it's me."

"You. Hi Louise."

She can hear him sighing. That's one thing most people don't realize about the phone: the person on the other end can hear even the tiniest burp and gurgle, can sense your attention wandering away and back. It's worse than talking face to face.

"Well, what is it?" her father says.

"I'm calling with news."

"Great."

"Are you ready?"

He doesn't say anything, so Louise plunges ahead. "We're getting married. Al and me are."

"Al and I, you mean."

Louise glances at Al, but he's examining his fingernails, his head bent so she can't catch his eye, make a face at him or give her father the finger. No good without a witness.

"Yes, Al and I. We're, um, engaged."

"Well, that's wonderful." His voice is heavy, but Louise thinks he sounds sort of happy. "That's really wonderful," he says again.

"Yeah," she says, trying to think what else to tell him. With him it's like playing Pick-Up Sticks, never knowing which motion will set the whole pile flying. "Is Mom there?"

"Well, you can probably guess where she is."

"Where?"

"Taking a nap."

"You don't think she wants to talk to me?"

"Hate to wake her."

"Oh," Louise says. "I guess I could call back." She thinks of her mother sleeping in her beautiful iron bed, the covers pulled up around her neck, safe from the world. She might be wearing earplugs to keep out the sound of the lawn mower.

"Sure," her father says. "And is Al going to write a letter?"

"A letter?"

"Yes."

"For what? To announce it?"

"Asking for your hand."

"I already gave him my hand."

"Oh."

"He's holding it right now." But Al is in the kitchen, whistling and running water in the sink, doing the dishes that have been piling up for days. He's probably figured out that it will be a long conversation.

"When I married your mother, I wrote her father a letter pronouncing my love for her and asking for her hand in marriage. That's what my father told me to do, and I did it. That's how it was done."

"Huh," Louise says. "How about that."

"To show respect for the family," her father says.

"I see."

"So, do you think Al will write one?"

Like she's a package all wrapped up and tied with a ribbon, a present to be passed from one person to the next. "Probably not," she says. It's best not to lie, or he'll be checking his mail daily, sifting through the envelopes anxiously, growing more irritated as time passes.

"That's a shame," he says.

"No, don't. Don't think of it like that." Louise tries to keep her voice from going high. She doesn't want to beg. "Times have changed."

"I live in the time I live in," her father says, and there's no arguing with that.

In Louise's favorite dream, she sits down to a gigantic supper with her family all around her. Al is by her side, passing the mashed potatoes and gravy, the green beans, the yeast rolls, all the food to the next person. Louise and Al are perched on taller chairs than the others, high-backed chairs with red velvet seat cushions and clawed feet. Almost as if they're king and queen. They look out over the table, and Louise knows that they own the table the way some people own countries. All the guests—her silent mother, her contrary father, Al's immaculate, expectant parents, Franklin and Moose side by side with napkins tied around their necks—must do as they say. If

Louise smiles, they all have to smile back. If Al takes a bite of his sweet potatoes, everyone else must follow. If Franklin or Moose swipes a piece of turkey from one of the other guests' plates, no one complains; the cats are the guests of honor, demanding nothing but a good piece of meat. In the dream, Louise and Al eat slowly, savoring each bite, safe in the knowledge that they can do as they wish.

———————

"This isn't working," Louise says. She slams down the phone and puts her head in her hands. She doesn't know why they've bothered to tell anyone. Al is right: the courthouse is an excellent place to exchange vows, and a whole lot cheaper, too. They won't invite a single relative. Afterward, they'll go on a long trip, maybe to the beach, where they'll find exotic shells and bury their feet in the sand.

"What?" Al says. He's still in the kitchen, drying dishes and putting away pots and pans.

"I said, my family sucks."

Al comes out of the kitchen, a towel draped over his shoulder. A dark water spot covers his shirt front, making him look like he's been wounded or is sweating profusely. "It didn't go well?" he says.

"My father wants a letter."

"Just like you said, huh?"

"No. A different letter, from you. Asking him for my hand." Louise holds up her hand and waves it slowly, as if she's setting off on a long cruise to a foreign country.

Al nods his head. "Which hand? Left or right?"

But this is no time to joke, and Louise doesn't even smile. "My figurative one. My hand in marriage."

"Oh. Well, we can't do that."

"I told him."

"And?"

"And he didn't like it. He said he wants what he wants."

"Same goes for us." Al twists the kitchen towel and pops it at the coffee table. He pops it at the chair with the stuffing hanging out and at the magazine on the floor. It makes a loud snapping sound, and bits of the blue shredded napkin fly off the table through the air. He pops Louise's knee. "Gotcha," he says.

"Quit it."

Al pops her other knee, and this time it stings a little. Louise jumps up and lunges forward, her hands clenched and ready, for what, she isn't exactly sure.

"Whoa," Al says, "them's fightin' fists. You weren't kidding." He takes a step back and stands, the towel limp at his side. He tilts his head slightly and considers her, and Louise knows he's seeing something new, some part of her that hasn't been there before. Sharp bones and mean teeth, maybe, or spikes coming out of her head, her true and shriveled self.

She doesn't say anything. She's thinking how close she came to punching him, jamming her fist into his open, questioning face. As if he's caused it all. As if he created her sullen father with his ridiculous demands, her mother, listless and still sleeping. And his parents, bright and cheerful, wanting no surprises, nothing unusual.

"Ma'am, I'll have to ask you to put down your weapon." Al's voice is thick with fake drawl, like the police officers on TV.

Louise releases her fists and lowers her arms. Her fingers are sore from being clenched so tight. She looks at Al, the gap between his teeth making him seem young and somehow more himself. "Sorry," she says. "I don't know what I was thinking."

"That's what everyone says, ma'am," Al says, and tips a pretend hat at her.

And Louise is reminded of why she is marrying him. He's light, light enough to carry her away like a hot-air balloon from her family, living underground and sifting through the dirt for flaws and bits of evidence that they've been wronged. The construction company, where she becomes invisible, the disembodied voice of a cocktail hostess. And her future, bland and flat and no help at all.

"Let's not call anyone else," she says.

"Right. We can order a pizza and play cards," Al says.

"Good. Fine."

It is the perfect solution, she knows, and for this second she feels as if she could solve anything, decisive, quick, no regrets. The kind of clarity that descends suddenly and is just as suddenly gone.

Louise gathers up pieces of the blue napkin, which are strewn all over the carpet. Franklin is chewing on a piece, tossing his head and making little growling noises.

Al picks up Franklin and pulls the paper from his mouth. It's dark with saliva. He rolls it into a ball and the cat watches expectantly, waiting for him to toss it so he can chase after.

"Throw it to me," Louise says. "Maybe we can teach him to play Keep Away." And she cups her hands into a bowl, waiting for the catch.

Locusts

In the summer the locusts spit on my arms when I walk down the street. It's not because I'm hurting them or because they hate me. They just don't know what I am. They see me coming and worry I'll put them in a bag and carry them home. They treat me like an enemy their own size, try to poison me with one drop. Sometimes I think it's raining and I look up at the sky, but then I remember that rain consists of many drops, all coming down at once.

I don't like locusts much. I read that they lay their eggs inside twigs, and when the babies hatch they fall to the ground, dig holes and burrow down like it's their own funeral. They stay there for seventeen years. All that time they suck on root juices, shifting around in the soil, finding the best roots. And when they come crawling out, they look around for their mothers, search for a drink of water, wonder what their names are. No one is there. The mothers have died years before. I don't know what happens to the fathers; the book I'm reading doesn't say. But I do not like locusts. I would not take one home and care for it. I would not talk to it and make it feel more comfortable. It is not my favorite animal.

The spitting, though. If I had that spit. Imagine what would happen if I used it on someone who pushed me down or bit me or called me a bad name. Think how this person would fall paralyzed to the ground, would die a few seconds later. Think of the surprise. My own killer spit. As it is, my saliva is only good for the first stage of digestion, and at night it also keeps my mouth from drying out if I breathe through my nose. Now that I'm fifty-two, it's hard to breathe quietly; Lucretia says I snore on purpose.

For a while, each night before I went to sleep, I concentrated on having saliva as potent as mace. I envisioned my victim covering his face, saying Ow ow ow hoo boy what is this stuff, and his words ran together, his ears shriveled, his eyes turned to prunes, he picked them out and ate them. His hands fluttered to the ground and landed palms up. I would act surprised, mumble something about a new brand of chewing gum, say a small prayer. The prayer went something like, Please make sure he has a good bed and healthy meals in heaven. Sorry, God, it was an accident.

The God part is not so much for God as it is for me and any by-standers who happen to be listening. They should be on my side from the beginning.

The first person I spit on was a young woman, probably in her mid-thirties, in the produce section of the grocery store. She was examining the lettuce, her eyebrows knit together, her teeth large and square. Her hands grasped each head and shook it lightly. I didn't want to hurt her; I just thought it would be good to practice. The way she frowned—as if choosing the best head of lettuce were a serious matter, as if it would solve everything. The way her feet pointed away from each other, the way she stood on her toes, her well-manicured hands. I could not help myself.

I have, it turns out, a natural talent for this kind of thing. I did not miss. My aim was true. Right on the neck. The woman absently reached her hand back to wipe the drop away. She did not look up. I waited for three whole minutes, and she did not. The lettuce drew all her attention. I decided I would have to practice more. I picked through the apples and felt for bruises, and I told myself, Martha, you just have to be patient.

My mother and father named me Martha almost by accident. Before I was born they spent months tallying a list of the names they loved. As they said each name, they must have imagined certain characteristics. For example, if I had been named Zill, the most beautiful name in the world, I would have a passion for skydiving and late-night walks in the rain. If my name were Em, short for Emily, I would have a penchant for canning homegrown vegetables, and I would be afraid of the dark until the day I died. And if I had been named Richard, well then, of course I would have been a boy.

But I am named Martha because one day when my father was driving down the road that goes to the next state, the list, which rested on the dashboard, flew out the window. It was summer, and my father leaned his arm out the window and whistled the first lines to all the songs he knew. He did not notice. My mother sat at home, holding her pumpkin belly with one hand and drinking a glass of water with the other. Neither of them noticed. Their precious list was gone forever. Their plans for the color of my hair, my likes and dislikes, the size of my feet. My ability to cook and draw and swim.

They must have scratched their heads, rummaged through the entire house for that scrap of paper. They probably tore their hair out. Maybe they wept, threw things. The list of my names lay in a puddle by the side of the road. But instead of starting all over, instead of trying to remember the twenty or so names, they looked at each other, crestfallen, and said, Guess we'll just have to name it Martha if it's a girl and Herb if it's a boy. And that was the end of that. I was a girl and Martha is my name. I have mop hair that used to be the color of pinto beans, and large feet, and crooked fingers that bend in several directions, and a good brain.

My brain has never given me any trouble, and I can say with certainty that if it had been me who had lost the list of names, I would have sat right down with a pen and tried to reconstruct it. I would go straight through the alphabet, and I would say to myself, A recalls Anastasia and Alyssa and Allerine, and B reminds me of nothing interesting and neither does C, but D is definitely Desiderata and Desdemona and Diamond Darling and Dahlia. I'd continue this way until I ran out of letters. And when I got to M, Martha would not come to mind as one of the better names.

It's obvious that in my sister's case my parents did not lose the list; she was born with good fortune. Her full name is Lucretia Miranda Cala. All her names end with "a," whereas only my first and last names did, before I got married. My middle name is Jane. This was part of the accident, also.

Lucretia is seven years older than I am. I will turn fifty-three in twelve days. Lucretia says I have had enough parties and that this year we will just sit in the front yard and sing the song to me and eat pound cake. We'll see. I've told Lucretia time and time again that pound cake tastes like moist cardboard, and that I want a small secret thing for a present, maybe a sparkly glass eye or a marble to roll around in my hand. Maybe a piece of luck, a horseshoe, for example.

––––––––

Lucretia used to have brown hair down to her waist. Her eyes blinked wide open and closed again; she was easily surprised. She fancied herself a joke-teller, a comedienne, and she told jokes to herself while she cleaned the toilet and dusted the furniture. She was never in love with anything. All her life things have fallen into her lap: good grades, invitations to fancy events, men with perfect eyes and valentines held anxiously behind their backs, her own house. As far as I can tell, she still cares little for these things.

Now Lucretia's hair falls out in the shower and while she sits on the couch. I find the long silver strands; sometimes they wrap around my arm or one of my toes. Always I am careful to hide them. They upset her like that, scattered throughout the house, intertwined with the shag of the carpet. She complains that she is going bald, that it's a sign of death. So I put them in the cat food bag since I am the one who feeds the cats and I know Lucretia will not look there.

––––––––

Every day I go to the grocery store. Lucretia sends me in the morning and at night, and each trip I pick up two or three items. We do our shopping this way, product by product. One day I buy frozen peas, paper towels, and apples, and another day I get chocolate pudding—Lucretia's favorite dessert—and a can of olives. I walk the three blocks to the Great American Food Store, past the small boy eating pill bugs, the four gray houses all in a row, the construction workers in their bright orange hard hats, the shuttered windows, the whirring locusts, the parked cars.

Lucretia points her finger. Out, out right now, she says. Go pick up some plastic wrap, a bottle of juice. Leave me. She says I wander around the house too much, click my teeth, wave my hands. But she imagines this. People see twice as much as they really see, their minds making up most of the pictures, changing colors, covering up shadows. I know this just like I know I have an ingrown toenail.

The yesterdays creep into my head, mice in the corner, twitching their fine whiskers, showing their teeth. Closing my eyes doesn't help. Neither does tapping my feet and humming Christmas carols. They ask, soft and shrill, Where are those yellow button-up-the-side galoshes you had when you were seven? Where is he, that bald-headed man, the brown plastic glasses on his nose, your husband? What was the first thing you learned after you were born? How do you know you look the same in the mirror as you do to other people, when you have never seen the color of your eyes and the shape of your nose for yourself?

When we were young, Lucretia used to give me things. People called her beautiful. Long limbs and a smart face. She did not need presents the way I did; people gave her more and she valued them less. For example, the time Albert Sanders gave her a rock shaped like an egg. Lucretia was sixteen, and our parents said she could go on dates. She dated Albert first: calm, nice, a moose, thick bodied and eager.

I came into her room once and she was sprawled on the bed reading, absorbing the words, her face very still.

"Can I see your egg-rock again?" I asked her. I liked to touch the smoothness. I liked the fact that Albert had found it in a field, that he had not bought it in a store.

Lucretia put up her hand to shush me, her palm flat as if she were directing traffic. "Wait a sec," she said.

She did not have any pictures anywhere. The walls were white and blank. Almost a motel room; anyone could have stayed in it.

Finally she looked up. Her lips were thinner than usual. "Over there," she said, "on the dresser by the mirror."

I picked up the rock. It was the size of a chicken egg, white flecked with gray. I rolled it around in my hand and rubbed it against my cheek. In the mirror I watched myself pretend to crack the rock in two, pour out the contents, scramble them up in a pan. I made gurgling, hissing noises, the sound of an egg frying.

"Shh," Lucretia said. "I'm trying to read."

I said nothing. I rolled the rock along the top of her dresser. I wished I had a smooth gift, a boy to ask me places. I wouldn't mind if he was a moose. Nine years old, my face plain as dough, I would not mind at all.

Lucretia slammed the book shut. "Just take it, Martha. Just take the stupid rock," she yelled. "Anyway, I don't even like Albert. A rock is a rock. You find them on the ground."

I watched, fascinated by the sudden transformation: one minute reading, the next furious. I paid careful attention to the way her face creased in anger.

"Take it. It's yours. It means nothing." She propped herself up on her side, opened her book, pretending to read again.

"Thanks."

This is how she gave me things. But somehow they were never as nice as when they had belonged to her. I wished I could leave them in her room, could go in to examine them from time to time as if they were pieces in a museum, on display.

The second person I spit on was a small boy, perhaps two years old, stringy blond hair matted with food. Again, it happened in the supermarket. His face was squinched, red from crying. He reached for his mother. On the floor next to the shopping cart lay a half-eaten cookie. The boy opened his mouth wide, filling his lungs with air to let out a howl or sob in a kind of terrible mourning. His mother faced the shelves, glancing over brands of raisins, perhaps, or comparing prices per ounce.

I could not bear the sound. I know I should have felt sorry, especially since a cookie must matter quite a lot to someone who cannot see over a kitchen table or tie a shoe. I know loss is proportional to possession, that it could be graphed on a chart by a famous scientist. But this boy bothered me. I gathered the spittle to the front of my mouth, walked slowly over, deposited a drop or two on his head. His mother turned around, a box of raisins in her hand. She gave me a concerned look, but she had not seen.

The boy stared at me. Mama, she drooled, he said. His voice, now that he did not cry, was high and wobbly. Nonsense, his mother responded. She scratched the side of her face, put the box back on the shelf. They continued down the aisle.

This day marked the third week in which I had spent at least an hour each evening developing my talent. At night I sat on the love seat and thought of cells with different skills, with super protoplasms and abilities to produce deadly chemicals. Lucretia read in the rocking chair. Every few seconds the back of the chair hit the wall. With each dull thump she said, "Sorry." This is what we did with our evenings.

But I had been thinking hard. I knew when the boy did not die that the food and leaves stuck in his hair must have saved his life. There was no other explanation.

I met Bartlet Johnson in eleventh grade. He had moved in with his Aunt Jessica because his mother had run away. No one could find her. She left in the night, and the next morning when Mr. Johnson planted himself at the head of the table, expecting his breakfast, he did not realize he had a long wait ahead of him. He sat for a full twenty-five minutes, got all the way through the news and sports sections of the paper, and still only the place mat lay before him. No eggs, no bacon. Mrs. Johnson left no note.

This was Bartlet's favorite story, the one he told most often. When I met him he was telling it. He told it the night of our wedding reception, all the friends and acquaintances standing in a cluster around us. Sometimes he said his father was a stern businessman who frowned and wore a great deal of black and navy; other times he was jovial, raw faced, the manager of a gas station, wearing a bowler hat to work in the mornings.

But always, his father decided Bartlet must go live with Aunt Jessica, his father's sister. And always, Bartlet said he thought his mother had gone to find her fortune. The country she went to varied, but the reason was the same. Mrs. Johnson no longer wished to attend the town Ladies Guild tea parties. She did not want to partake in Sunday afternoon dinners. The hill country did not suffice. She planned to see the ocean, a mountain or two, but no more flatland.

I first saw Bartlet leaning against a stop sign, hands pushed down in his pants pockets, legs so long and gangly they looked as if they wrapped around each other three times. It is true that his skin had a yellow pallor, that his hair already receded from his seventeen-year-old forehead. He coughed periodically and had the nervous habit of rubbing the thumb and index finger of his left hand together, brushing off invisible particles. Three or four kids stood around him. As I approached, it looked as if the kids were paying homage to road signs. But it was Bartlet, voice low, emphasizing the importance of the story, of what would happen next.

This time his Aunt Jessica, whom we all knew as Mrs. Culver, was a witch. All through supper the night Bartlet arrived, she had pretended to play the piano on the dining room table and would only speak to him when he stared at her. She chanted to herself every night, muttered things under her breath, wore dirty aprons, raved about baked beans. She had eight cats and they all bit. She said reading was the devil's pleasure. She would not let Bartlet draw pictures; she claimed it was voodoo. She had eyes that flashed green in the night but remained dull all day long.

About his mother, Bartlet said only a few sentences. She had gone to find her fortune, probably in Australia but who knows, maybe Canada. She had black hair with a little bit of gray. She knew how to play the flute.

Bartlet's father had a long nose. He wore a brown bowler to work. He liked bacon for breakfast.

We stood there transfixed, gathering his words like marbles, stowing them for future reference. Bartlet's Aunt Jessica ranked among the most popular and highly respected women of our town; our mothers invited her to every luncheon they gave. To imagine her wandering the house in filthy aprons, talking of voodoo and the devil, thrilled us to no end. We waited for Bartlet to tell us more. But he shut his mouth into a straight line, crossed his arms, and just stood there under the stop sign a few feet above his head. Tom Jasper invited him to his house for a game of football. I continued on my way home.

So, really, the first time I met Bartlet he did not meet me. I remember this and wonder if it means anything, the way a horoscope or a fortune would.

One day a few months after Bartlet disappeared, Lucretia showed up at my house. When the doorbell rang I was brushing my teeth, and I had to spit out all the paste fast and wipe my mouth.

"Coming," I finally yelled. I nearly tripped over Bartlet's old golf clubs laid out in the middle of the living room floor. Every afternoon I examined the contents of the closets—I liked to rearrange the objects by shape. The day before, I had begun to put all my long, thin belongings in one closet: mop, broom, candlestick holders, vacuum cleaner, tarnished coat rack.

I looked through the peephole. Lucretia was itching one of her ankles and did not see my eye through the hole. I opened the door. "Oh, hello!" I said. "I didn't know you were coming. Is everything okay?"

Lucretia stood up straight. She nodded. "You've got a fleck of white stuff on your chin." To show me, she pointed to a place below her mouth.

"Thanks."

I wiped the toothpaste away. Lucretia peered past me into the room, taking in the golf clubs, the sofa against the wall, the coffee table where it belonged.

"May I come in?"

I moved to the side and followed her into my own house, watched her stop and sniff.

"I'm roasting a chicken for supper. Would you like to stay?" I said.

"No, thanks. No. I was just in your neighborhood, you know, taking the bus to that coat store up the street. Winter's coming." She stretched her arms and yawned. "Well. Nice seeing you." She smiled, but I saw she was staring at the golf clubs.

"You don't want to stay?"

We hadn't even sat down yet. We'd barely made it past the foyer into the living room.

"I've got to catch the bus back."

And then Lucretia turned to leave, brown leather handbag draped over one arm. She walked briskly across the lawn and out to the street, her steps careful and dignified.

These visits happened again and again. Lucretia arrived, stayed a few minutes, then said she had to go before I could give her anything to eat, before we had a chance to say much of anything. Sometimes she just asked me questions. Why didn't I have any photos of Bartlet anywhere? Why had I moved all the furniture into one room? Did I rearrange my house every day?

But now that we live together at her place, I no longer have to answer. Five months of staying alone was enough, Lucretia said one day. She said I would be better off living with her. At Lucretia's house the routines keep us silent, which she would consider an improvement. The living room is always a place for reading and watching television, and the pictures on the walls are all paintings, no photographs, no one we would recognize and talk about. I go to the grocery store, Lucretia reads, sometimes we take the bus to other parts of town.

Bartlet did not have handsome eyes or graceful hands. He was a terrible dancer. He only loved me for a few minutes, long enough to ask me to marry him and wait for me to say yes. Then in a few days we were married, just like that. We were together for sixteen years.

He called me Mar instead of Martha. I wanted to tell him to feel free to call me Zill, but somehow I never got around to it. I did not love him the way I love thunderstorms or the middle of the night. But I loved all his stories: the way his father turned into a different man every day, the fact that one week his Aunt Jessica was a millionaire with connections to British royalty and the next she had such a bad memory she could not recall her last name. Bartlet's eyes gleamed as he talked. His face grew sharp. He looked past me as if he were watching a movie.

He hated children and cats. He thought camping was silly. He could not eat dry cereal without vomiting. He demanded bacon and eggs for breakfast, just like his long-ago father before him. He was afraid of the dark. We had to sleep with the bedside light on. I wore eyeshades. He gave me the same present for my twenty-ninth and thirtieth birthdays—a manicure set. His face grew yellower with the passing years. The years passed like stones.

Lucretia never married. She planted a garden, taught third grade, sold her vegetables, bought herself a house. She giggles at her own jokes and does not care whether anyone else finds her funny. Her favorite joke is a pun, where the words mean something else. She also likes useless sayings. For example, she loves it when people say, He's feeling under the weather, or, She can't see the forest for the trees. Everyone knows, Lucretia says, that there are no forests around here. And it is impossible to be under the weather, especially since one can never see the weather, but only what it is doing.

She does not like slapstick, however. She doesn't think it's funny when I fall down in the garden or on my way to the grocery store, although I find this particularly amusing. It's as if my feet have a mind of their own—of course, Lucretia would at least find this, the saying, funny—and even though I tell my feet to take a step or two forward, they disobey. So I find myself gazing at the sky when just a second ago I saw parked cars and the end of the street. But this only happens once in a while, hardly ever, nothing to pay special attention to. Myself, I like the cartoons they have on television, the ones where the characters skid or slip on banana peels and yell "Whoaaaaa." I like the way they run into walls and fall down stairs even though they are trying hard to watch out, to take care.

———

The second time I met Bartlet, the first time he met me, I told him I was sorry. I had seen him ahead of me on the sidewalk and had run to catch up with him.

"What for?" he said. He was carrying a bag of groceries home to his aunt.

"For your mom running away. And I'm sorry your aunt's a witch. She looks fine to me."

"Yeah. She looks fine to everyone. But I know because I live there. That's the trick. Living there, you see a lot more."

I walked next to him toward his street, the silence between sentences neither awkward nor comfortable. It had just rained, and steam rose up from the asphalt in slow curls.

"So, what's your name?" he said, peering in the bag. "I can't believe how much Kleenex my aunt buys."

"Martha."

It was then I realized he did not remember me from the stop sign meeting. This didn't bother me, though. I knew I did not have his caliber of stories. No one in my family had run away. We all still lived in the same house, four of us sitting in the same chairs each

27

night at supper, Lucretia a teacher now, our parents still our parents, me continually worried and in high school.

"Oh," he said, his face blank and neutral.

"My name's an accident. It could have been something better. You shouldn't judge me by my name."

But he wasn't listening. "Look at that dog," he said. "It's hurt."

I looked. Mrs. Gibson's dog, old and fat, limped across the street. "Probably a thorn in its paw," I said, then tried to call it over. "Here, dog. Here." I took a few steps toward the animal, but it stumbled off in the opposite direction.

"I'm Bartlet," he said.

"Yeah, I know."

He turned, surprised, then rubbed his fingers together.

"We met," I said. "By a stop sign a few days ago." I put out my hand and we shook. His palm felt rough, dry, the skin of an orange.

I know I did not love him, but he was easy to listen to. It seemed as if I would be able to love everything else but him all at the same time.

Always I imagine Lucretia in a blue fancy gown, the material crisp and shiny. It's a picture I carry in my mind: my sister with thin white arms stretching to encircle the world, her skin healthy, no regrets. She holds many things: a tin of chocolates an admirer has given her, the future tied in a ribbon around her wrist, a grocery receipt, a small mirror shaped like a heart. I watch her laughing, head thrown back, mouth open. She laughs and laughs, so happy with a joke she has just told herself. I carry this picture everywhere, and when I actually see Lucretia I'm surprised that she looks so different, in jeans, wrinkles around her mouth and under her eyes, hands on her hips.

My mother did not have any boy babies, just me and Lucretia. I once asked her if she wanted a boy and she shrugged. She said it was the luck of the draw. I never had any children myself, not while I was with Bartlet and definitely not after. I didn't want them eating all my food and stepping on the spider plants growing in the living room. I didn't want to worry about their fragile bodies getting hit by cars or tripping down the back stairs. And I didn't want to wash their clothes. The only thing is, now that I will turn fifty-three in twelve days, it would be nice to have some relatives coming to my party.

Bartlet will never return. I've been waiting eighteen years now, time enough to be born and become a legal adult all over again, or, if I were a locust, to drink root juices under the ground for seventeen years before arriving in the world.

An evil person stole Bartlet right off the porch. One evening during the summer he sat on the front steps to eat an apple. When I went out to see if he wanted to watch some television with me—it was how we passed the time in the evenings—he was gone.

His matchbook and cigarettes lay on the top step, so I thought he had ventured around the block for a walk. Not that he had ever liked walking before, but there were his cigarettes, one poking out of the pack for good luck. People don't just disappear and leave their cigarettes behind, I told myself. He'll be back in a few minutes, I said. And, a few hours later, I thought, He better get his little pear face in this house right now.

Finally I called the police. They told me not to worry. An Officer Rochester said they couldn't do anything until morning anyway, since I had no proof that Bartlet intended to come right back inside the house as soon as he finished his apple. This officer didn't believe me for a second, I could tell. He thought I had soft brains and a worrying nature, that I wrung my hands constantly.

In the book I have been reading, it says when locusts reach their full size they can fit into a rectangular box. Insect scientists, who study this all the time, have created a formula to find the normal surface area of the locust. If the insect, with wings and legs carefully plucked, is fit snugly into a box, its surface area should equal one-half that of the box.

I cannot imagine how this practice contributes to scientific knowledge; in order to be measured, the locust has to die. I think of myself dead and ready to go in the coffin, not fitting because my arms and legs are still attached.

But still, these locusts. I can't trust them for a minute. Last week as I was walking down the street, one spit on me so hard I fell down. I scraped my knee and both my palms. Lucretia doesn't believe it was the locust. She says I tripped on a rock or a crack in the sidewalk. She says locust spit isn't poisonous anyway, even though I have read parts of the bug book out loud to her. And last night when I told her how I tripped, she just laughed at me. I didn't see a pun in any of the things I'd said, and when I asked her what was funny she covered her mouth as if she were coughing.

I pulled one of her hairs out of the couch cushion and held it up to the light. "Oh look," I said, "I wonder whose this is." A breeze shifted the air, and the silver hair moved slightly.

Lucretia shook her head. "You are always trying to use my hairs against me. But they don't matter. They used to grow out brown. Now they grow out white." She smiled, all her yellow teeth in a row. "Just shove it down under the seat and I'll deal with it later."

I wound the ends of the hair around my index finger. "Too thin. Awfully thin for a hair," I said, examining it in the light. And then I slid it back under the cushion like Lucretia told me to do.

Lucretia bumped the back of the rocking chair against the wall. "Sorry," she said, like always. Outside, the locusts rubbed their wings together, furiously singing to the night.

I didn't always think I would be a wife with a husband who disappeared and a sister who loves puns. I thought I would fly like Amelia Earhart: thick airplane goggles, leather jacket, fur around the neck. Planes to land, oceans to cross. Red wool scarf and a strong handshake.

Instead, after Bartlet disappeared I guarded the house. It had a couch and easy chairs and a coffee table. It had curtains and a teapot and a window fan. Bookshelves, pictures on the walls, matching silverware, a radio. Two quiet goldfish. Everything settled, calm. The hum of the heater in winter. I felt as if I were someone in a photograph: I am Martha and this is my backdrop. I cannot move my arms; they seem to be stuck. I wandered the rooms, fished hair balls out from under the bed and placed them under the dining room table. I shoved Bartlet's neat piles of magazines to the floor. I sat on the couch and picked at my fingernails.

Bartlet sold hats downtown in his very own store, which he called Johnson's Hat Store after his last name. Businessmen came in during their lunch hour to buy the newest styles, studying themselves in the mirrors that covered each wall. Bartlet said men did not like to let others see them catering to their own vanity, and if they did not have to turn their heads to find their reflections, but only had to stare straight ahead, they would usually buy the hats. Bartlet said this was the difference between men and women. I told him men were all the more vain for not being able to admit it.

Sometimes I helped him unpack new shipments in the stockroom. White hatboxes with the brand names etched on the lids in gilded curlicue lettering, the smell of leather, velvet, felt. I stacked the boxes in piles maybe six feet tall around me. Once I accidentally bumped one. The boxes tumbled down, crashing and hitting other boxes. Bartlet came running in, said What is it, what is it, hand mopping sweat from his forehead. But when he saw the boxes scattered all over, some of the corners bent, he shook his head slowly and closed his eyes. He squeezed and unsqueezed his fingers.

"Mar. Mar. Mar." I watched his lips say my name, pursing, pushing off each other, opening. "This mess, this mess, the boxes you damaged. Probably forty or fifty."

"Sorry," I said. "I didn't mean to."

"Maybe you should go home and never come back."

He said it as if he could not decide, as if he were discussing whether or not it would rain, whether or not the corn would be good this year.

That was the last time I was in the stockroom. I went in the front sometimes to bring Bartlet the lunches he had left behind on the kitchen counter. Out in the store his stride quickened. His keys jingled in his left pants pocket. Once I even heard him humming, low and almost melodic.

When I moved in with Lucretia, she let us get a cat. The animal is fat and very calm. We found it in Lucretia's backyard one afternoon. It would not leave. It just lay on its back with its paws in the air as if it were an actor playing a dead thing.

We think this cat belonged to someone else before it came to live with us; it does not scratch the furniture or jump on the table and eat the dinner off our plates. And it is polite — except that when it arrived it was secretly pregnant. We did not know this until we found the babies squirming and mewing in the potato bin. Three we gave away and one lives under the house. At night we hear it stalking mice. We call it Ida for no reason.

The way that first cat arrived, the way it played dead, I thought it was Bartlet in disguise. I waited for it to impersonate other things — a rock, Mrs. Johnson, a dog, Aunt Jessica. But that was just the way it slept; it was not acting at all. Then I began to think that perhaps, just as this cat had arrived — by accident, not even walking, just waking up in a new place — so had Bartlet found himself sitting on someone else's front porch, apple still in hand, cigarettes and matches left behind.

I couldn't decide whether I should begin knocking on people's doors in nearby towns, asking if they had seen Bartlet, or whether I liked living with Lucretia and the cats, going to the grocery store every day. And I didn't know what I would do if I found Bartlet eating someone else's supper, selling hats in a different Johnson's Hat Store, telling the same stories to someone else.

Yesterday I spit on Lucretia. We will both never forget it. I went to the grocery store for some lentils; Lucretia wanted to make fifteen-bean soup, but we only had fourteen kinds in the house. I bought the orange ones because they were on the shelf. A sunny day, the grocery store nearly empty, a Monday with everyone at work. My favorite cashier, Janet, who never wears her name tag, rang up the lentils.

"The store looks very clean today," I said. The cashiers like it when I tell them this.

Janet smiled, her braces showing even though I know she hates to wear them; in fact, she often talks without moving her lips. "Thanks, Martha. Frank mopped the aisles this morning." She handed me my receipt. "Have a good day."

When I got home Lucretia was soaking most of the beans in the soup pot.

"Here you go," I said, handing her the bag. She opened it up, peered inside, drew out the package.

"They're orange."

"Yeah." I walked over, stood behind her, examined the lentils. They looked fine. "So?"

"I need the brown kind. I told you brown. The recipe says brown lentils." She spoke slowly, as if she were arranging the words before me.

I couldn't remember if Lucretia had said brown or orange. I just knew she'd asked me to buy lentils. "I don't think you said either way. That's the kind Great American carries. The only kind. They probably taste the same, anyway."

"But they won't be the same. Otherwise the recipe wouldn't have specified. Ruined, possibly ruined."

She turned away and opened the package over the sink. A few lentils scattered on the floor.

"You don't have to use them."

She glared at me. "Might as well," she said, her eyes slightly narrowed and her lips pursed, a look she had perfected years ago. Maybe the day I was born. Maybe as soon as I could see and remember. It's hard to say.

The earthy smell of beans absorbing water filled the kitchen. And then I had to do it. Brown lentils. It was just a color, nothing more. My older sister, always the beautiful one, her long hair and self-made career. The hundreds of books she had read. Her life cradled in her own hands. A marble to guard. I gathered the saliva and spit hard. The drop landed on Lucretia's forearm. Her sudden look of horror, her mouth open, curled down a little with disgust.

"See, I spit on you. There it is," I said.

Like the other times, this spit had no poison. Just the same old spit cells producing the same watery stuff. But Lucretia's face, the degree of offense, her hand holding a spoon in midair, as if she would either strike me or drop it to the floor.

I stood taking in the meaning of what I had done. I had spit on my sister. Meanwhile, slowly, methodically, Lucretia pulled a piece of paper towel from the dispenser above the sink and wiped away the splotch on her arm. Then she folded up the paper towel, square upon square, creasing each fold, shaking her head. "I would never do such a thing," she said. "I would never spit on you. I just wouldn't."

Still I did not know what to say. "Oops," I managed.

But "oops" is never enough. "Oops" implies an accident but probably doesn't even exist in the dictionary. It's just not impressive. Yet I couldn't bring myself to say I was sorry either—that I would never do it again, that I did not mean it.

I went outside and sat on the front steps. Ida rubbed against my leg and purred. Across the street the boy who ate pill bugs rode his tricycle along the sidewalk, ringing the bell attached to the handlebars. His short legs pedaled furiously, thin bones, matching outfit. I imagined my own self flying over the countryside, no longer sharing Lucretia's house, my hands on the controls, red scarf flapping in the wind.

Bartlet and I sat on the double swing in Aunt Jessica's front yard. It was July. Tent worms spun their massive webs around tree limbs, choking them and turning the leaves brown. Locusts droned, melancholy in the heat. We rocked back and forth on the swing, Bartlet dragging his feet on the ground. He began the story of the songs his mother used to sing to him.

"She had this awful voice, so the songs never made me sleepy. They made me laugh." He looked at his hands, rubbed his fingers together as he would countless times in the years to come. "And when I laughed I didn't mind the dark. Of course, the night-light stayed on. I still needed the night-light."

I nodded, trying to look serious. I was eighteen, my hair pulled back and tied with a blue ribbon. I considered myself on the verge of wisdom and great insight. Bartlet kept talking, his words filling up the still summer air.

"When she sang happy birthday to me, my father would look over at her and frown. She sounded that bad. But they would both end up laughing, and then we would eat the cake."

I searched my mind for something to add. "My uncle is tone-deaf," I said finally. "He was born that way."

"What?" Bartlet looked at me, confused. We rocked back and forth in the swing, neither of us saying anything. I wondered if he

34

had forgotten I was there. I was supposed to be his girlfriend, but sometimes I felt as if I were just part of the scenery. Bartlet would have been happy to tell his stories to himself.

"How's your Aunt Jessica?" I said.

Bartlet wrinkled his face in disgust, then wiped away the beads of sweat forming on his upper lip. "You should see her. Lately she's taken to calling the broom her lover. She says, 'The broom, my love, come dance with me, sweep me off my feet.' And then she giggles hysterically. She turns to me with the broom in her arms and says, 'Meet Bartlet. He's my nephew.'"

I nodded and kept my face neutral. If I asked too many questions, Bartlet might lose his train of thought and I wouldn't get to hear the rest. It was all I wanted, to hear the rest.

"And the other day she puckered up her lips and gave her hand a big kiss, and then she smeared it on the broomstick. I couldn't take it. I left after that." He rolled his eyes. "A loon. That's all. A gray-haired loon."

I sighed. "Too bad," I said softly. "Tragic." And we sat the rest of the evening, me sighing and nodding while Bartlet slowly widened the circle surrounding his tiny kernel of truth.

Dogs

Celia wants a new puppy more than anything. Her family already has a dog named Casey, but he's old and he smells. It's not a terrible stink, but she can't nuzzle her face in Casey's fur or scratch him too hard—the sour skin smell will rub off on her hands. And he's got a flea allergy that makes him chew off all the hair on his butt and lower back. When he wags his tail his whole rear sways and he looks like a bald man shaking his head. Her family has had Casey ever since Celia was little. You and Casey grew up together, her mother likes to say. You were babies together, but now Casey's old and wise and you're not even a teenager yet. Her mother is always explaining that dogs age faster than people—seven times as fast, in fact—and Celia should remember this when she plays with Casey. Don't be hurt if he's slow fetching a stick—it takes him a while, her mother says.

Celia tells her mother that Casey should have a puppy to play with. "Maybe he needs to be a father," she says one day while she is watching her mother clean out the roof gutters. Her mother wears her father's red and black checked wool shirt, bright against the sky, and moves slowly along the edge of the roof.

"Why would he need that?" her mother says. The rake scrapes against the gutter and leaves fall to the ground in big clumps.

"He'd feel responsible. He'd have someone to take care of, and it would make him think he was young."

Her mother purses her lips and tosses down a pecan. "Catch. It looks like it might be good."

Celia sticks the pecan in her pocket. "He would feel young," she says again.

"I think his feelings would be hurt," her mother says. "He'd feel like he was being replaced." Her hair falls forward when she looks down, and all Celia can see is her mouth. She is smiling, and Celia knows this means her mind is made up. It is the kind of smile that seals the conversation before it veers off toward argument.

———————

At night Celia thinks about the puppy she would have. It is all black with a short broad nose and shiny eyes. It has a pink tongue that sticks out when it pants. She cannot think of a name yet—she knows the minute she sees this dog, a name will pop into her head, but for now she just likes to think of it as The Puppy. She tells it secrets, wishes, worries, everything. It does not tell her anything back, but she knows the puppy understands. It sleeps curled up by her neck and follows her to the end of the walk where she waits for the car pool to pick her up for school. It loves her best. She thinks of the puppy every night as she is falling asleep, and sometimes, when she is almost out, she thinks she can hear it scrabbling around outside her bedroom window.

And in the mornings Celia hears Mr. Farlan, the next door neighbor, getting his dogs ready for a walk. Celia's bedroom window looks out onto Mr. Farlan's driveway and the gate to his backyard. He is old and round. His belly sticks out, but not loose, not flabby: stout. He wears thick glasses that magnify his eyes, make them look gray and wide. He looks a little like a baby, the way he stares, but it is only the black plastic glasses.

Mr. Farlan almost died of a stroke a few years ago, and he had to get a bunch of dogs to help him stay alive. He takes all five of them walking now, each on its separate leash, early in the morning and just before supper. They bark and jump, give off high-pitched whines when they hear Mr. Farlan coming with the leashes. He jingles the leashes like giant keys. Some are made of chain, and two, for the little dogs, are made of leather. Celia likes to say the names of the dogs to herself: Prince, Lacey, Wallace, Junior, and Tulip. Prince and Wallace are the littlest, some kind of terrier or poodle, maybe. Celia doesn't know all the names of the dog family, but she knows these two.

Here Prince, Mr. Farlan says. Lacey, you bad girl, quit chewing that milk jug. He opens the gate and they come bounding out, sniffing at the ground and jumping up on their hind legs. Off we go, down, down, he says. Finally he yells Calm down! and amazingly they quit their yelping. They do listen to Mr. Farlan, guardian of dogs. They sit quivering as he snaps the leashes onto their collars. Celia peers through the venetian blind, careful not to open the slats too wide. She doesn't want him to know she watches every morning from her bed.

Then they head down the driveway and around the block, fighting for the lead and walking zigzags while Mr. Farlan tries to maintain a steady pace. Celia can see that it must be good exercise to keep those dogs in line. Lacey and Junior are enormous mutts; they yank their leashes taut. When Mr. Farlan is out of sight, Celia lies back down and pulls the covers over her head. She likes to inhale her own breath. The air around her grows warm and damp, no light shows through, and she falls asleep again. When her mother wakes her for school, she feels groggy and impatient, as if she has been interrupted in the middle of an important dream. She wishes, sometimes, that Mr. Farlan was her grandfather. With his round belly, his wide eyes, all those pets like children, she thinks he would be perfect.

Celia's father is making notepads for her tenth birthday party. She's giving them away as favors. He cuts words and pictures from magazines, old cards, newspapers, and glues them around the edges of each page. He says he will make a master copy, and then get the pads made up at a print shop. Celia would rather give away kazoos or coupons to the local ice-cream parlor, but her father says no, this is a lasting gift. While he works, his mouth settles into a straight line. "Hand me those scissors, will you?" he says, and barely looks up. He has spread out all the scraps of paper on the dining room table. Celia gives him the scissors.

"This is going to be great," he says. "I hope we can get the original to the copier in time."

"You've got two weeks," Celia says.

"But the shop might be booked with other jobs. We want plenty of time."

Celia sighs. "I still wish we were giving away something simple."

"It's not a simple party. A treasure hunt, make your own pizza, make your own party hat. This is going to generate tons of creativity." Her father pastes down a quotation by a poet named Walt Whitman.

"Very well then, I contradict myself. I am large . . . I contain multitudes," Celia reads out loud. "I don't get it. Multitudes. Nobody's going to get it, Dad. They won't even know how to say the words."

"They'll save them. And years later, they'll be like souvenirs. Think of it. They'll say to themselves, 'This is from Celia's tenth birthday party.' And they'll remember the party, and what it was like to be ten."

Celia gathers some scraps from the table, scrunches them into a ball. Her father is enjoying himself. Bits of paper are scattered on the floor and in his lap. As she leaves, she hears him mumble, "I should have been an artist."

Celia is playing campfire in the front yard when she sees Mr. Farlan coming home from his afternoon walk. The dogs lag behind him now, tongues hanging out. Celia digs a hole in the ground and puts sticks across the top, edge to edge, to form a kind of grill. Then she places big oak leaves on top; this is the food. She rubs her hands together and pretends to warm them over a roaring fire.

"Hello there," Mr. Farlan says.

Celia waves.

"What'cha doing?"

She looks down at the hole, the sticks, and knows it is too hard to explain. "Playing a game."

"By yourself?"

She nods. Mr. Farlan probably hasn't noticed that there aren't any other kids on this block. It's mostly families like his: older people with pets.

Mr. Farlan unhooks the dogs from their leashes and they bound across the front lawn. "Get back here," he calls, "get back on your own property. That ain't your front yard." He opens the gate to his backyard. They all run through, except Prince, who stands at the edge of the curb, considering the street.

"Prince," Celia calls, and he looks over at her, startled. She is not, after all, his owner.

"Come on over, Celia, and I'll get you a cookie." Mr. Farlan is out of breath from his walk, fumbling with the key to the front door. "Mrs. Farlan made a batch this morning."

"Wait," Celia says, and runs inside her house. She wants to give him the ceramic dog she made in art class. They have been playing with clay, as the teacher calls it, although Celia would rather think of it as pottery. She molded a dog sitting on its haunches, almost begging, its face turned toward the sky. The best part was painting on the glaze; it didn't change color until the piece was fired. She packed on the thick, clear liquid, no idea what shade of yellow it would turn out. Everyone around her dribbled similar liquids on their pieces—bowls, ashtrays, pencil holders, butter dishes—from bottles labeled magenta, onyx, lavender, burnt orange. They were hopeful, imagining the colors they would see. Celia's resting dog came out bright yellow, bright as fake sunshine.

"Art should have a place of honor," her mother said, and placed it between the bottle of vitamin C and an avocado pit sprouting its roots into a jar of water.

Celia grabs the dog from the kitchen windowsill. She hides it under her shirt until she is out of the house. Her mother might be working at the library today, but she isn't sure. Celia gave the sculpture to her just a week ago. It won't look good to be giving it away again.

When she gets to Mr. Farlan's front door, she holds the sculpture behind her back and rings the bell. She sees his balding head peek through the curtains, and then he is at the door.

"Come in," he says.

Celia enters the living room, breathes the stale air, the vague smell of mothballs and different foods built up over time. The rest is impulse. When Celia thinks of this moment years later, she will feel embarrassed and a little sad at having seemed so desperate, so clearly beyond the bounds of the normal and proper, the realm of good taste.

———————

In Mr. Farlan's living room, Celia sits on the plastic-covered sofa and tries hard not to move and make the plastic crinkle—it reminds her of a baby bed, plastic under the sheets. She bites into a cookie, and it is delicious, just the right softness, not too many raisins. She looks around, sees the pastel portraits of Mr. and Mrs. Farlan hanging side by side in matching frames, Mr. Farlan with lots of dark hair and his wife without her glasses. She can tell they were nice even in the years before they got old. And then Celia cannot help herself.

"Mr. Farlan," she says, "would you be my grandfather?"

He looks at her, his eyes larger than usual, the same startled expression Prince had when she called him by name.

"I mean, my pretend grandfather. My real ones are dead." She wipes her hands on her shorts and folds them in her lap.

"I already have grandkids," Mr. Farlan says.

"It could just be pretend. I could come visit like I am now, and tell you things."

He nods. "I see," he says. "But it wouldn't be true."

"But I need a grandfather. I don't have any." Having ventured this far, Celia cannot stop.

Mr. Farlan winks. "We could be friends, I guess. That would be all right."

She smiles. "We already are friends."

"We could be better friends." Mr. Farlan is picking dirt from his fingernails. This surprises Celia. She cannot imagine cleaning her nails in a room covered in plastic. All she can think is that Mr. Farlan is going to get in trouble. She must be making him nervous.

"Okay," she says, before he can go back on such a mild agreement.

"I guess that'll be fine. All my family—Mrs. Farlan, the grandchildren, my dogs, and Celia. That's fine."

"Good," Celia says, and hands him the ceramic piece. "Here. I want you to have this. I made it at school."

Mr. Farlan takes the sculpture from her and turns it over, holds it up to the light. "Thank you," he says. "Did it take you a long time?"

Celia shakes her head. "No. I might be an artist when I grow up. My dad wishes he was an artist."

"What kind of dog do you think it is?"

"It's supposed to be a golden retriever, but the glaze came out wrong. I didn't know it would be so yellow."

"Well, thank you," he says again. "Now I have a golden retriever. All kinds of dogs in this house, all kinds." He puts the dog on the side table next to the couch. It is the brightest thing in the room.

Celia fails her math quiz and her father offers to explain long division to her. "Once you learn it, you'll never forget," he says. "Just like learning to breathe. You never have to think about it."

Celia can't imagine long division being as easy as something you don't even realize you're doing most of the time. "There're too many steps," she says. "And the teacher goes too fast. I can divide and subtract at the very beginning, but then I get stuck."

"When we're done, you'll be able to divide anything the long way." Her father pulls a bunch of napkins out of the holder on the table and looks around for a pen. "Do you have something to write with?"

Celia gets him a pen shaped like a candy cane from her school bag. She's not supposed to use anything besides a pencil in math class, but she writes notes to people with this pen.

"Okay," her father says, "we'll have one lesson, and then we can toss the baseball out back." He bought Celia a left-handed mitt last year, and in the evenings they throw the ball back and forth. The most difficult pass is through the bars of the swing set—they call this the Monster Obstacle. The dogs next door bark and run the length of the fence, chasing their voices. Celia thinks they can't figure out the sound of the ball smacking the mitts, and this alarms them.

"Deal," Celia says.

Her father loves numbers. It's beyond him that anyone would have trouble understanding math, would be afraid to have the numbers come out wrong. His help sessions go on for hours, it seems. Sometimes they make her cry, all the numbers he writes on the scrap paper. She wants to memorize the steps, but he won't tell them to her. You should be able to reason them out, he says.

By the end of this session, her father has covered most of the napkins with equations. Celia can divide, subtract, carry, and divide again. But she cannot decide what to do next—she sees all the numbers under the hook, the lines drawn across, and she gets lost. "Step by step," her father says.

"Which step? How can you tell?"

"It just makes sense," he says, and folds the unused napkins diagonally into triangles. "When you know, you know."

Celia has had enough. "Where did you put the ball and mitts?" she says.

"In the garage, on the workbench."

"You go get them," Celia says. She is afraid of the garage in the evenings. Even before it gets dark, the garage is shadowed and musty. When she turns on the light by the door she can hear animals scurrying—probably only roaches, but Celia doesn't want to see them. "I'll meet you outside by the swing set."

She cannot wait to get away from long division.

———————

Sometimes when Celia and her father play catch in the backyard, Casey howls and howls. He howls the way dogs will if an ambulance or a fire engine passes through the neighborhood, howls as if the sound of pitching a baseball back and forth tears at his eardrums. And yet he ignores Celia when she fills his water dish or when she calls him to come in.

Celia stands twenty feet from her father, and Casey insists on lying exactly halfway between the two of them. He watches the ball and paws at the ground and howls. And Mr. Farlan's dogs pace the fence on the other side. Celia and her father call it the Dog Jungle. "Playing baseball in a jungle of dogs," her father will say, raising his voice to be heard over the din, "trying to overcome the Monster Obstacle."

"Pack of wolves," Celia says, and throws the ball high above her father's head so he has to jump to get it. "That's out, you would have been out," she says every time he misses. Her father throws the ball back, always right to her outstretched mitt.

"I was never good at this," he mutters, and Celia tries to imagine what it's like to be on the end of one of her throws, how it feels to catch one. She wonders if she throws hard—the ball makes such a solid sound.

———————

The day of Celia's tenth birthday party approaches. Her mother has said she can pick all the hiding places for the treasure hunt. Each girl will get her own set of clues, one clue leading to the next, and in the end—behind chairs or lodged in bookshelves or in the freezer—

they will find the notepads her father has made. She hopes they will be surprised, happy. She hopes if they are disappointed, they'll hide it well. Her father will be watching. Then they'll eat the little pizzas they have garnished with their favorite toppings and maybe tell ghost stories or act out the latest movies.

Celia wants to invite Mr. Farlan to her party, even though she's pretty sure he won't come. She can just imagine the way he will say no, shaking his head a little, smoothing the plastic covering on the couch. He'll be glad, she thinks, that she bothered. Now that they're friends. It's the thought that counts. She knows he will never fit in with all the fourth grade girls. He'll have a terrible time.

When he is getting out of his car, his arms full of groceries, she says, "Coming to my party next week?" She sees, sticking out of the top of a bag, a carton of ice cream, which she knows is bad for strokes. She decides not to say anything.

"What's the celebration?"

"I'm going to be ten." Celia leans against his big gold car, an American model, plenty of room. "There's going to be a treasure hunt and make your own hats."

Mr. Farlan nods his head, wipes a little sweat from his chin. Even in October it is hot, Indian summer. His car must not have air-conditioning. "I'll see. It sounds like fun."

"It will be. One o'clock sharp. You don't have to bring a present." Celia says this because she has heard her mother say it to the girls in the school car pool.

"I beg your pardon." Mr. Farlan smiles. "I'll bring one if I want."

"Okay." This is fine with her—the more presents the better. Maybe he'll give her one of his dogs. "See you there."

He waves. "See you."

The guests will arrive in a few hours, and Celia has to help her mother straighten up the house and vacuum. Her father is gathering magazines from every room for the hats. He says the girls can cut out the pictures and paste them on, collage style.

"I wonder," Celia says within earshot of her mother, "if I will get a puppy. It's all I want."

Her mother laughs from the kitchen. She is sticking candles on

Celia's cake. "Wish again," she says, "and while you're at it, refill Casey's water bowl and bring him some Scooby snacks."

Celia sticks out her tongue and shakes her head, even though her mother can't see her. She hates the way her mother calls the dog treats Scooby snacks. She can tell by her voice that she thinks it's somehow funny, maybe even a little cute. "I just changed the water yesterday," she says.

"Do it again. Would you like to drink water a day old?" Her mother sticks the last candle in the middle of the cake. "A dog needs lots of attention. It has to be taken care of."

Celia pours out Casey's old water, which has two flies and a leaf floating on its surface, and fills the bowl with water from the garden hose. Casey lies in the sun by the swing set, his pink back soaking up the warmth. Celia's mother doesn't like Casey to lie in the yard; she's worried he'll get sunburned, all that bare skin, so little fur. Try to talk Casey into lying on the back porch, she tells Celia sometimes, as if you could talk him into anything.

"Here, Casey," she says. "New water. Water, water, on the porch."

Casey doesn't even look up. He's resting his head on his paws and appears to be surveying the garden.

Celia tries again. "Casey Casey Casey. Here, old hairless."

It is useless. He doesn't even respond to insults. She leaves the bowl on the porch and shuts the screen door to keep out the flies. Time to help her mother hide the treasure clues and blow up balloons before all those girls arrive. She wants everything to go well, as smooth as the parties she has been to at skating rinks or bowling alleys—the matching napkins and cups, the song, the feeling of organization, perfection.

———————

The girls arrive in twos and threes, carpooling even to this party. They come running up the front sidewalk, holding their presents out. When Celia opens the front door to let them in, they hand her their packages, which are mostly small and rectangular. As Celia takes each one she thinks, This is a book, this is another book. This is a jigsaw puzzle. She can tell by the presents that it's true, these girls think she is a brain at school, always raising her hand to answer questions, turning in her spelling tests and times table quizzes first.

They have no idea that she can't do long division. None of them knows her well. She wishes she had some best friends, some people to climb trees and play kickball with. These girls like jacks and trading fluorescent-colored shoelaces. Even though she hardly ever plays with them, they are the closest thing Celia has to friends.

No one hands her a puppy. She expected this too. She knew that no matter how many times she announced that a puppy was the best gift, the girls' mothers would have to check with her mother first, and she would laugh and say no, no, they already have a dog named Casey.

But there is the treasure hunt, and then they will each make their own hats, and when Celia looks around the table, preparing to blow out the birthday candles, she will see these girls in their green and red and yellow cone-shaped construction-paper hats, and this will please her.

———————

Celia's mother is slicing the cake when the doorbell rings. Celia looks around the table. All the girls are there, not counting Lucy Morrow, who is in Dallas visiting her aunt, and Angela Baker, who simply said she couldn't come, didn't even give a reason. For a second Celia wonders if it could be Mr. Farlan, but she has not really expected him, especially now that the party is about to end.

"I'll get it," her father says. He has been taking pictures of each stage of the party with his fancy camera, which he carries around his neck the way a photographer would. "Don't eat any cake until I come back. I want a picture of that, too." He goes to open the door.

Celia hears him talking to someone, but she doesn't recognize the voice. She peers through the kitchen to the front door and sees an old man, bent and trembly, leaning on a cane. Even though it never gets cold in this part of Texas, he wears a hat, round with a brim like she's seen in black-and-white movies.

Her father stands next to the man. He speaks softly and turns his back to the table, maybe to avoid a scene. But the man steps past Celia's father while he is still talking and walks into the dining room. He pauses and looks around the table at all the guests. He stares longest at Celia, who sits at one end, a pile of presents next to her on the floor.

"Wait a minute," her father says. He is fiddling with his camera, removing and replacing the lens cap. "Just hold it."

"I see I've interrupted something," the man says, and points his cane at Celia. "It doesn't matter though. Not for a family of animal abusers."

Celia's mother stands up at the other end of the table. She is about to hand Celia the first piece of cake. "Excuse me?" she says. She waves the knife from side to side, as if she's forgotten she's holding it. "Who are you?"

"Fellow next door sent me." The man tips his hat. His hair is a dingy yellow with streaks of white. "Put that knife down, please."

Her mother sticks the knife into the middle of the cake so hard two of the candles fall over. Some of the girls giggle. "I asked who you are," she says. "I expect an answer. We're having a party at the moment, and I'd like a little courtesy."

"Let me see your dog," the man says, not a bit intimidated. "I hear it howls and doesn't have any fur. You pick it off yourself, lady?"

Celia's mother's eyes widen.

"You have a dog, don't you?"

"You mean Casey?"

"That its name?"

Celia tries to think who lives on the other side of them. Until a few months ago, the house was empty, and she's never met the people who live there now.

"Where are you from?" Celia's father says.

"Born and raised here, a San Antonio boy."

"No, I mean, who do you represent?" Her father has taken off his glasses; his face is red.

"I volunteer for the city. I check out cases like yours." The man taps his cane on the floor and says to Celia, "Happy birthday."

"I can assure you, you've made a terrible mistake," her father says. He is trying to reason, to make sense, the way he does with numbers. "I'm sure we can clear this up."

The man laughs. Girls begin to shift in their seats. Alice Quinn leans over to Jen Weeks and whispers something, and they both laugh.

"Yeah, we can clear it up. We'll take away that poor dog, give it a real home."

48

Her father walks toward the den, nods his head for the man to follow. "Watch yourself," he says. "You know nothing about us. You're beyond your bounds."

"Nonsense." With every other step, the man taps his cane along the floor. His shoulder blades stick out like wings. He walks slowly, looks all around. "Your neighbor, now, there's a man who knows how to take good care of dogs. He's got five himself."

Then Celia knows. Mr. Farlan can hear Casey's baseball howls better than any other neighbor.

As the door closes, Celia thinks she hears her father curse under his breath, but she can't be sure. She looks back at the table, at the knife stuck in the cake. She thinks of the puppy she's wanted, of filling Casey's water dish, of his bald, bald back. She feels like maybe she should lie down.

"Who was that?" Jen Weeks asks.

Celia shakes her head. "I don't know."

"How can you not know?"

Celia wants Jen to shut up. She sounds excited, as if this were some kind of adventure.

"Where's the dog?" someone else asks.

Celia shrugs.

Her mother pulls the knife from the cake and wipes it off with a napkin. Lemon filling oozes from a big hole in the middle. "Let's sing the birthday song again," she says. "Let's see how loud we can sing."

While the man and Celia's father talk, her mother rushes the guests through the treasure hunt. "Hurry, hurry," she says, "whoever finds their treasure first gets a prize." Celia cannot imagine what this prize could be. They haven't planned the hunt to be a contest—the pleasure was supposed to be in the seeking and finding, not in speed.

While the girls search, Celia's mother pulls her aside. "I'm going to give the winner a bag of chips."

"What?" Celia says. This is not a normal kind of gift. It's a snack food, something kids bring to school in their lunches. "What kind?" she asks.

"I thought potato chips," her mother says. "It's the only kind we have. Unless you can think of anything better."

Celia can't. All around her, girls are unfolding scraps of paper, running to different rooms, reading their clues out loud. "Fine," she says. "The winner gets chips."

Alexa Zinser finds her notepad first. "'Very well then, I contradict myself,'" she reads. "Neat." She pushes her long hair back from her face and begins flipping through the pages. When Celia's mother presents her with the family-size bag of potato chips, she says thanks and keeps reading her notepad. Celia wishes her father were through with the man so he could see this. Alexa even knows what "multitudes" means. Her mother teaches English at the university. Celia can tell that, for Alexa, this is the best part of the party. It doesn't matter, though. She wishes the guests would take their notepads and hats and extra pieces of cake, and just go home.

––––––––––––

After all the girls leave and Celia helps her mother throw away paper plates and half-eaten pieces of cake, she sits down next to her father on the couch.

"Hey, birthday girl," he says, and puts his arm around her.

"Who was that guy?" Celia says.

His name is Mr. Steele, her father tells her. Mr. Farlan sent him to inquire about all the howling and Casey's ugly skin. He told Mr. Steele they were neglectful and possibly mean.

"He walks in on people in the neighborhood all the time," her father says. "He does it constantly. He thinks he's a one-man branch of the Humane Society." He shakes his head. "I told him he was severely mistaken. Torturing Casey, can you believe it? I said if I ever saw him on our property again I'd take him to court."

Celia nods her head. She imagines her parents in a courtroom, all dressed up, holding a chart of Casey's illnesses.

"I don't think you should play over at Mr. Farlan's anymore," her father says. He is flipping through a leftover notepad, admiring it. He stops and nods when he gets to certain pages, pleased.

"I won't," Celia says. "Don't worry." She isn't worried about Mr. Steele's reappearance. What bothers her is the idea Mr. Farlan must have been carrying in his head the whole time she's known him, even when she gave him the sculpture and they agreed to be friends: her family is cruel and uncommonly bad. Maybe she should have looked more closely at Mr. Farlan's eyes when he talked. Those glasses are so thick—they could hide anything.

"—no need to tell them about it," her father is saying.

Celia hasn't been listening. "Huh?"

"You don't have to tell anyone about this mess. It's no one's business, especially since it's all a misunderstanding."

"Okay." Celia smiles now. She's on the outside looking in at the way her father sees her: young, easily placated.

He traces the outline of the large question mark he pasted next to the Whitman quote. "A waste," he says, half to himself. "What a waste."

Celia doesn't care about the notepads anymore. They seem frivolous, absurd. She pats her father on the shoulder, says nothing.

Then she goes out to the backyard to visit Casey. He is basking in the sun as usual. Today he lies on his side with his legs stretched out, as if he tipped over and just stayed that way. When Celia walks up to scratch his neck where his collar rubs, he lifts his head and yawns. Celia tries to imagine her family the way Mr. Farlan sees them—hurting Casey on whim, because they can. The images won't come. Of course he is wrong. Sure, she has wanted a puppy—something younger, more playful—but that doesn't mean she has betrayed their dog, does it?

Casey makes the small grunting noises that mean he's happy. Her mother calls it Casey's purr. He rolls over onto his back and Celia scratches his speckled belly for a while. His right leg jiggles and his tail thumps the ground. He smells terrible, the way he's smelled for years, a thick, pungent odor. The vet says it's part of the allergy, part of being sick. Like the way people get bad breath when they have a cold. Casey grunts and Celia scratches him. She wonders if he can tell she thinks he's too old, that she's wished for a younger dog.

———

Days pass and Celia does not speak to Mr. Farlan. She closes the venetian blind tight against the sun and the sound of him taking his dogs for their early-morning walks. She makes up mean stories about him: how the couches are covered with plastic in case he pees on them, how Mrs. Farlan forces him to wear a diaper, how he spies on all the neighbors and poisons their gardens. The more she hates him, the less of a betrayer she is.

When she finally ventures over to Mr. Farlan's house, she has begun to think of it as forbidden, even haunted. The mesquite trees in his yard seem shriveled, and it has been weeks since the lawn was mowed. She raps hard on the door and looks around his front porch while she waits for him to answer. All the potted plants are dying. They haven't been watered in a while. The dirt is cracked and riddled with brown crinkled leaves—further confirmation that he poisons gardens.

When Mr. Farlan answers the door, she is bent over a large pot, pulling out all the dead leaves and putting them in a pile. "What are you doing?" he says. He doesn't open the screen door, as if she's a stranger.

"You're killing all your plants," Celia says, and stands up. "You have to remember to water them. Plants take a lot of responsibility."

"It's fall. They're going to die anyway when it gets cold."

Celia nods. The hallway behind Mr. Farlan is dark, and all she can see is his face. "Were you sleeping?"

"No."

"Good."

"Do you want to come in?"

Celia shakes her head. "I'm not allowed to come in ever again." She pauses a moment to let this sink in. She wants it to hurt.

Mr. Farlan turns the knob on the door back and forth. It makes a small squeaking sound. "All that wasn't about you," he says.

"Yes, it was." She makes her voice stern and low. "I need my sculpture back."

"Sculpture?" His face is blank.

"The yellow dog I gave you, remember?" How can it be that he doesn't? "You'll have to give it back."

"I'll look for it and leave it on my porch. Come back in a couple of days."

Celia nods. "Don't forget. And don't break it. I need it."

"Right," Mr. Farlan says. His eyes look wide and young as always. She can't tell anything from his face. He gives a little wave and shuts the door, and Celia is left on his porch surrounded by all his dry pots. She stamps her foot on the pile of dead leaves, and they crumble into dust.

———————

Celia is reading at the kitchen table. Her mother is at the sink washing the dinner dishes and humming. Soap suds fly off her hands and the dishrag and land on the floor. She washes vigorously, with enthusiasm.

Then she stops. "Hey," she says, "where's that dog you made at school?" Really, it is amazing that she hasn't noticed its absence, in the countless evenings she has stood there.

"I don't know," Celia says. She is caught off guard, mesmerized by the book she is reading about four children who run away to live in a boxcar. "I'll look in my room. I was playing with it a few days ago."

"Such great art," her mother says. She wrings out the dishrag and drapes it over the faucet. "I hope you haven't lost it."

Celia turns her head aside. "No, I'm sure I didn't." She folds down the page of the book to mark her place. "I'll be right back."

"That would be a shame." Her mother shakes her head and begins humming again.

Celia will have to sneak out into the night to get the sculpture. But she can't take the flashlight from the kitchen drawer. Her mother will notice. She will have to be quiet, clever. She's not supposed to be out after dark. Her father is engrossed in a public television special on the language of dolphins, and he doesn't look up when she slips behind the couch and out the door. She can hear the sound of the ocean on TV, and she knows that her father will fall asleep watching, as he always does.

———————

The night is cool and a little windy. Leaves rustle in the trees and skitter along the street. The air feels good on Celia's face. Fall has finally come. She doesn't feel right running through Mr. Farlan's yard anymore, so she walks in the street to the edge of his sidewalk. No one is home. The whole house is dark, and Celia can't see the way to the door. She walks slowly. Her feet hit pebbles and small sticks, which skip along the cement. When she gets to the steps, the dogs begin barking wildly, ferociously. She is a stranger to them now.

They hurl their bodies against the fence. Their five voices sound like a hundred; they are large and strong as wolves. Repent, repent, they bark, and Celia thinks of how she has hated petting Casey, has detested his pink skin, his sour smell, his age. Neglect, cruelty.

At the top step, Celia runs her hand along the porch floor, hoping to find the ceramic dog sitting patiently, staring upward still. All she feels is grit and crumbled bits of leaves. The dogs howl, long and high-pitched, almost echoing. She has never been afraid of them before. Now she is certain they will come for her. They will jump the fence any second and barrel up the steps. The latch on the gate rattles and shakes with the weight of the dogs hitting against the fence. Surely it's rusty, about to break.

Celia does not wait to find out. She forces herself to walk down the porch steps one at a time, her arms stretched out in front for some unseen obstacle, before she sprints to her yard. She nearly trips over the hedge that divides her family's property from Mr. Farlan's. She stubs her toe on one of the sprinklers sticking out of the lawn. Finally she reaches the front door. Her lungs feel like they are closing up. She wonders if she has forgotten to breathe, despite her father's promises that such a thing could never happen.

Now the dogs sound far away. Through the window she can see her father sprawled out on the couch, his feet dangling over the armrest. Dolphins leap across the TV screen in slow motion. Calm down, Celia, calm down. It is something Mr. Farlan would say to his dogs. She tries to control her breathing, puts a hand to her face, which is hot and probably pink. She stands still, hopes for composure. Her toe throbs, and she wiggles it to make sure it isn't broken. She knows she will never get that sculpture back. It is Mr. Farlan's now. It is his forever. She feels a hundred years old, her whole life spent. Her parents cannot help; no one can.

She yanks the door open. Her parents haven't heard her come in, and, for a moment, Celia can look around her house as if it were someone else's, the living room of some other, different girl.

Pampas Grass Day

Dark, it was getting dark when their father left them standing next to the driveway and the pampas grass, the tall one, the middle one, and the shortest. Their names were Axle, Luce, and Jake, and they were sisters and brothers three. They stood for a while, pondering, looking, careful not to run their fingers the wrong way up a blade of the pampas—it would take a section of skin easily, the blood running onto the wrist. Axle stood tall and straight, her face spotted with those growing-up sores, that acne, her ears sharp in the way a fox's ears are sharp. Luce had her baby doll, its white blond hair tufting through even, circular holes in the scalp. And Jake twisted his fingers together until they looked like two claws. His lips protruded downward. He was the youngest, and he had the smallest teeth.

"What are we doing?" Luce said. "Why are we here again?"

"Because," Axle said, "they're not getting along," and she wished she were an ostrich girl, her neck long and spindly, swiveling to the left and the right. She would wear a red scarf to cover the pink, mottled flesh, a thick red scarf with fringe on each end.

Jake bit his lower lip and turned to Axle. "Well, get us out of here because I don't like it one bit." He wanted to play inside and rub his hand over the cool, smooth wood of the banister.

But their father had left them there by the driveway to the right of several patches of oil, such a leaky car, someone should fix it. They could hear the voices rising inside, their mother screaming, Shut up, shut up, their father yelling as usual, You may make a great mother but you're a whore of a wife.

"Go stand by the pampas grass in the side yard," their father had said. "We don't want you hearing everything." They stood with their knees locked, the sun setting before their eyes, the early evening of summer.

"The days are getting shorter," Luce said.

Axle nodded. "Soon we'll have to go back to school."

The pecan tree shifted slightly in the breeze, and they could see the new nuts, green and pinched, dangling from its branches. In the fall the nuts would be strewn across the ground, and their mother would give them old grocery bags with instructions to fill them to the top. There might be pie, there might be muffins.

The backs of Jake's knees grew sore with the constant pressure of his still body. He wiggled his legs quickly from side to side as if he were doing a dance.

"Let's play a game," he said.

Luce shook her head. The dark brown hair flew out around her face in thick strands. "We can't. We're supposed to stay here."

If she were at the drainage ditch at the end of their alley she could throw sticks into the water. They would float, spinning slightly, into the huge dark tunnel. Rats lived there, big ones with darting eyes. Don't go too close to the edge, her mother said, I'd hate for you to fall in.

"Maybe we could play a game right here, without moving too much," Axle said.

Jake nodded his head. "Maybe."

He and Axle looked at Luce. A stationary game would require all three of them, no bad sports, no yelling to distract their parents.

"All right," Luce said. "There's nothing else to do. We might as well."

They dropped to the pavement, still warm from the afternoon sun. They sat Indian style, their elbows on their pale, bony knees. Jake's little potbelly stuck out from under his shirt. He stretched the shirt over his stomach and tucked it into his shorts. Axle pressed her fingers to her face, feeling for new pimples, a nervous habit, disgusting, her mother told her.

"Crap on a stick," Luce said, "I just squished a pill bug." She cursed often. She put the Baby Tenderlove in the middle of their circle and brushed off her hands.

"I don't want to hear about it." Axle stared at her fingernails, jagged and bitten to the quick. "What game are we going to play?"

"Spit hand, spit hand," Jake said, suddenly excited, his face animated, his small teeth and red gums showing when he smiled. He pulled in his cheeks, gathering a bit of saliva to the front of his mouth. He spit into the palm of one hand and rubbed the saliva into the palm of the other, like hand lotion.

"Now," he said, "do this." He pressed both hands, palms down, into the cement, as people do when they finger paint or make a print of their skin, the paint smearing thickly, leaving small telltale ridges and wrinkles on the paper: the life line, the love line, the number of children they will have. When he lifted his hands up and away, rubbed the grit on his shorts, Axle and Luce bent forward. A thin outline of Jake's hand faded into the evening heat. One moment they could see it, the next it was gone.

Axle nudged Luce in the ribs. "Your turn. You go next." She stared at her own hands. "Maybe you should use more spit so the print lasts longer."

Luce spit four times into her hand. Her saliva was thick and clear; a little stuck to her chin.

"Messy," Jake said. "You're a pig mouth."

Luce placed her hands down, fingers splayed, clawlike. She held them still for a few moments, making sure the saliva would show on the driveway. "You watch it, Jake, or I'll spit on you." Like their mother, her hands were too small for her body, the fingers stubby, stunted.

"Aha," Axle said when Luce finished. "See how dark your hands are. See how much longer they last than Jake's. There's that scar from when you lost part of your finger in the car door." She traced her sister's print. "It looks like a fossil."

The sun began to disappear behind the house across the street. Soon it would be truly dark. The mosquitos would hover at their faces and ears, especially Axle's. Their high-pitched whine would give them away and some would be flattened against the skin, some flicked aside. Sometimes when Axle played in the city swimming pool she pushed all her hair forward so it hung down to her mouth. Then she twisted it until it stuck out straight like a unicorn horn. She bobbed around in the shallow end, buzzing. I'm a mosquito, she said, I'm a mosquito. She was odd for twelve, awkward looking, awkward acting.

"My turn," she said. She held her hands on the cement the longest of the three. It had become a contest—whose print stayed the darkest, was the most detailed, looked the most like the actual hand.

Jake smacked a mosquito on his calf. "Hurry up, Axle, you don't have to hold it there all night. Once you do it you do it, or you're cheating." He wiped the mosquito on the cement next to Axle's hands.

She lifted them. "There. Look. You can see all my joints, and there, you can see my callus."

"That's bull," Luce said, "there's no way any kind of callus is in that print." She shook her head and snatched Baby Tenderlove out from the center of their circle. "No way."

"Look." Axle pointed to a vague, half-formed splotch. It could have been anything.

"Where? I don't see anything. You know I won, mine was the best. You said yourself you could see my scar, you said it looked like a fossil." Luce laid the doll in her lap and folded her arms across her chest, skeptical.

"It doesn't matter anyway," Jake said.

Inside, something metallic clattered against the door. Their parents were talking lower, the words inaudible but forceful.

"I don't see why we always have to go outside when they fight." Luce leaned back and placed her arms at her sides, using her doll for a pillow. It hissed as the air in its body escaped. "Seems like we're out here all the time."

"They think we can't hear them, they think we won't know there's trouble," Axle said, flicking at a mosquito above her eyebrow.

Their mother had owlish eyes. She rarely raised her voice and instead sulked quietly, mumbled to herself, Go ahead, do what you want, you know how I feel about it. So Axle or Jake or Luce, whoever it was, felt guilty but went ahead and did the bad thing anyway. Their father often said he should have married someone else. I should have married the woman I met before your mom—we were in love. Beautiful, he said, but she wouldn't have me. Their father drank 7-Up at supper every night, straight from the bottle, and he never shared with any of them. No, he said, pulling the bottle close to his chest, you kids need your milk.

In the dark, the pampas grass swayed with the breeze. Wispy bits of frond floated down to the pavement and danced across the drive-way. The locusts hummed their night song, softer now that the sun had set.

"Jeez, when are they going to be done?" Axle said, not to ask a question but to wonder out loud.

No one knew when they would be done, when their father would open the screen door and stick his head out into the light of the porch. No one knew when he would say, his voice nonchalant, You can come in now.

"Never." Luce sat up, untied her saddle shoes. Four times her mother had tricked her into buying saddle shoes. Look at those, she would say while they were in the shoe store picking up different styles, turning them over, poking the soles and sticking their hands into each shoe as if it were a puppet. Don't you like these? her mother asked every time, her voice cajoling. I used to have a pair when I was your age. Tricked, four different times, and when Luce got home she hated the shoes, white and black and clunky on her feet. They looked like nurse shoes, and she was not a nurse.

"Well," she said, "maybe we should play another game." She glanced at Jake, who was picking his nose. "Jakey, quit it."

Jake closed his hand into a fist, didn't answer. Luce might tell, and even though their mother probably wouldn't care, it would em-barrass him.

"Maybe something other than that spit hand thing," Axle said. "Something more exciting, some kind of dare game."

"Well, you go ahead and choose it," Luce said, impatient. Some-times she told Axle what to do—Axle hardly ever acted like the old-est, even though she was.

"Okay." Axle bent her head into her chin. "Let's play pampas grass day."

"I never heard of it," Jake said.

"It's new." Axle leaned forward. "I made it up just now." She got up, stretched her arm into the pampas grass, turning her face away so she would not choke on the cream-colored fronds at the top of each sinewy stalk. She bent and twisted three blades, each several feet long, until they broke.

"Here, one for each of us." She handed one to Jake and one to Luce. "Watch out, they're sharp."

"What do we do?" Luce waved her blade in front of her face, back and forth, as if she were hypnotizing herself. "How do we win?"

Jake placed his across his legs.

"Careful, Jake, it really is sharp. Here." Axle reached across and put his blade on the ground next to him. And then she began to explain. "Well, you know how pampas grass can cut you if you run your fingers the wrong way, up the blade instead of down it."

The other two nodded. Every time their father pulled the car too close to the pampas, they had to get out on the other side to avoid brushing against the blades, thin and far reaching, almost as tall as their father.

"Okay, so it's a dangerous game. The object is to show your guts." Axle held up her blade, placed her thumb and index finger at the base of it. "You run your fingers up the pampas."

"It'll cut us. That's no good," Luce said.

Axle nodded. "That's the point. In other countries they play this all the time, like truth or dare, only better."

"I don't want to," Jake said. He folded his hands in his lap as if he were in church, as if he were praying, trying to be still, invisible.

"If you want I'll go first," Axle said, compromising, proving her bravery.

"Go, go ahead." Luce waved her hand.

Axle pulled her fingers up the blade quickly. It looked as if she were cleaning off a skewer or a knife, maybe with a dishrag, maybe with a paper towel.

"Okeydokey," she said, and even in the dark they could see several drops of blood falling to the pavement. Luce and Jake scooted a few inches back, resettled themselves. They did not want Axle's blood on their feet.

"The mosquitos will be worse now. They can smell your blood, they'll know where to find you," Luce said. She thought mosquitos were the same as vampires, miniature and more abundant, but otherwise the same.

"Wrong," Axle sang, "you're wrong. They find you by your breath, they can smell your breath. I read it in school." She pressed her index finger onto the cement. "There," she said. "That'll stay. It won't dry up the way the other hands did."

She looked at Luce. "Are you going to go or not? Maybe I'll be the only one with a real print, like one of those criminals. They're always getting their fingerprints taken."

Luce did not answer. Across the alley, Mr. Farlan's dog, Prince, began to bark frantically, jumping against the chain-link fence, landing, jumping again.

"Something's in our alley," Jake said. He stuck his thumb in his mouth, sucked pensively.

"It's nothing. It's probably just a cat. Prince hates cats. Remember how he got out that time and chased our Talleycat and we had to throw sticks to get him out of our yard?" Luce had even thrown a rock, but it missed. Talleycat liked her the best of the whole family. Their father had brought the cat home one day. This is my cat, he said, but Luce was still its favorite.

Without announcing her turn, Luce ran her fingers along her pampas, squeezing hard. "Ouch," she muttered, and pressed her fingers together, shaking them a little so the blood would drip. "I bet this is sharp as a razor." Once she had run her fingers across her mother's razor, the one she used to shave her legs. She had not known it would cut away a flap of skin, hadn't even felt any pain, but the cut bled and bled right through the bandage.

She placed her thumb and index finger on the cement as Axle had done, alongside Axle's fingerprint. "So," she said, "one, two, three—two fingers and a thumb. Your turn, Jake."

"No." Jake did not care for bravery. He wished he could lie down in his bed with the covers tucked tight around his feet.

"Do it or we'll tell," Axle said, her voice low. Of course there was nothing to tell. The house was silent; only the living room lights were on. Their parents might be having a civil discussion or they might be sitting silently, begrudging nothing.

"Yeah, Jake, you'll get in trouble with Dad," Luce said.

Axle tried to make her voice persuasive. "C'mon, don't you want your print next to ours? We can see them in the morning when it's light. They'll still be here."

"Okay," Jake said, wavering. And clumsily, he ran one finger along the blade.

Luce sighed, grabbed his hand, felt it for blood. "No, you didn't do it hard enough. Again."

So again he tried, this time closing his eyes. He was doing a bad thing. He wasn't supposed to hurt himself on purpose; it didn't make sense.

"Good," Luce said. "Now press it down quick, before it stops bleeding."

Jake held his hand down, fingers splayed, as if he were reaching for something. He licked his finger, the print made, the ordeal over. "There," he said, "clean as a whistle." It was something their mother said after she mopped the bathroom. He held his finger in front of his face, signing the number one in the dark.

"Well, that's that," Axle said, folding her hands in her lap. They held still, patient now to wait.

From where they sat they couldn't see the moon. It dangled high over the other side of the house, somewhere just above the vegetable garden. Every spring their father bought thousands of earthworms to replenish the soil. He kept them in a special trough for a few days, waiting for the right weather, overcast, damp, so he could shovel them into their new home under the ground.

"So here we are," Luce said.

"Um hmm." Axle jiggled her left leg and then her right, keeping those mosquitos, their pointy heads, their swollen bodies full of blood, from landing.

Jake leaned over, rested his head on Luce's shoulder. He stuck his thumb in his mouth, and soon his sucking was the only sound in the night air.

In the dark they sat. It might go on this way for the whole summer, their father sending them out every few evenings while he and their mother yelled, talked, did whatever they did. In the fall they would trudge to school carrying new bookbags and wearing those saddle shoes tied tight. Tomorrow morning they would eat their cold cereal with a teaspoon of sugar mixed in. And then they might check their prints in the driveway, the blood brown and crusted, looking mostly like thin smudges of clay.

Pressure

June's father is taking his blood pressure again. He takes it ten times in a row every day and records it in his running log. He's training to do a marathon, he says. "I'm in excellent health, but after all, I am in my late fifties. One can never be too careful. Blood pressure and heart rate can be iffy."

June and Stew are visiting. They said they would come by for a little dessert, but neither of them expected Simon to pull out a home-use blood pressure gauge. This is new. He must have bought it on impulse at the Olmos Pharmacy around the corner. Bargain of the century, he'd say. Couldn't pass it up.

"I'm glad you're being careful," June says, taking a bite of lemon pound cake. "It's not like you can feel your pressure rising, from what I hear. It creeps up on you." This isn't the right thing to say—it will only encourage her father to monitor his every change. But it's the best she can do. She can never tell how these visits will go.

Simon sips his Red Zinger tea. "Mmm, have a go at it." He passes the blood pressure gauge across the coffee table. "And you, too, Stew, if you want. Both of you are welcome to try."

June takes the gauge, which is heavier than she thought—the nurse always slips that thing on her arm as if it weighs nothing. There is a bulb coming out of a small box with a screen on it, and then the velcro cuff she's seen before. She's not quite sure how to put it on. Stew is dabbing at cake crumbs on his plate with his index finger. He doesn't look up.

When she tries to wrap the pad around her arm, Simon sits forward. "Wait. You have to roll up your sleeve first," he says. "It can't read through cloth. And you should be able to fit two fingers under the cuff before you start pumping."

June nods. She rolls up the sleeve of her dress and wraps the cuff around her arm, which looks pale and unnatural. She squeezes the bulb until the machine beeps, then sits as still as she can. She has watched Simon take his pressure three times already tonight, and every time he sat so still he looked nearly asleep. After a few seconds, the machine beeps a bunch of times and numbers flash across the screen.

"Let me see," Simon says, and comes around to her chair. Even Stew leans over from his chair to get a peek.

"One ten over sixty," June says. Her arm feels a little numb, and she wiggles her fingers.

Simon nods his head. "Ooh, that's good. I can hardly ever get mine that low. I swear, I'm almost asleep if I get something that good."

Stew clears his throat. "I think I'll get some more cake." He starts to get up and nearly knocks over the TV tray holding the coffee and cream. He grabs the tray just in time.

"Good catch," Simon says. "You sure you don't want to take your pressure? It's interesting. Really. But you should probably sit for a few minutes first. I always find that helps."

June hears a hint of condescension in her father's voice, as if he doesn't think Stew's pressure will be low enough. True, Stew doesn't do much in the way of exercise, but he's fine.

"No thanks." Stew is already heading for the kitchen. "I've got good genes for this kind of thing, and I get checkups."

"You don't think I upset him, do you?" Simon says. "I mean, it's just interesting, that's all, to see what your body's doing, don't you think?"

"Sure." June gives a half-nod. She doesn't want to take sides. She tries to envision the day when Stew and her father will become friends, maybe discuss a book they've both read or even see a movie together, but it's not likely. Stew must remind Simon of her mother. They are both quiet. It's one of the things she likes best about Stew and her mom: they listen more than they talk. With Simon it's just the opposite. In this way her parents must have been perfectly matched for a while. Simon talking and talking, and her mother quietly nodding, until one day she said, That's enough.

June was there, and she can name the day. It was just five years ago. They were eating breakfast. Simon was explaining his theory that women should take classes on how to become better wives. He said certification should be required, a diploma in the domestic arts. Alice banged her fist on the table, and all the dishes clattered. A Cheerios box fell over. June and Simon watched, amazed. June had never seen her mother make any kind of fist at all. They're divorced now. Simon once said that her mother's silences were a trick to condemn all his ideas; her lack of enthusiasm quashed them. She castrates me with silence, he insisted.

Stew comes back with another piece of cake. He takes a big bite, ignoring the fork on his TV tray. "Good cake." His mouth is full and it's difficult to understand him.

"Thanks," Simon says, and smiles. "Betty Crocker." He stretches his arms over his head and leans back against the couch. Above the couch is a picture of him finishing his most recent race, his face twisted into a grimace, arms pumping furiously. June can tell he's sprinting because he's a little blurry while the trees and the finish line banner over his head are clear. The photo is grainy from being blown up to poster size.

She tries hard to think of something to say. If she chooses the right topic, Simon will expound until it's time to go home, and she and Stew won't have to say anything. The conversation may be one-sided, but there won't be any arguments. Stew puts the last bit of cake in his mouth. She can hear his jaw popping every time he chews. He needs to go to the dentist.

They mean to get checkups, but it seems like they never get around to it. They are broke. Simon's teeth are bad from not going for years before June was born. When she was little, he would show her all the gaps in his mouth and say, "I didn't go to the dentist. And look what happened to all those teeth. Gone forever." June could see the spaces and the remaining teeth, some darkened and leaning in. She would rub her fingers across her own teeth to make sure they were still there.

It's so much money, though—fifty dollars just for the cleaning.

And God knows what else they'd find. June's boss at the flower shop even brushes her teeth at lunch. She bends over the sink where they cut the stems and scrubs with great concentration. June should be doing this, but she can't remember to buy an extra toothbrush to carry in her purse.

"—so if you don't want to, I believe I will," Simon says.

"Huh?" June hasn't been listening.

Stew looks over at her. "He's going to take his blood pressure again."

"Oh, sure. Go right ahead." She gives him the gauge. "Once is enough for me."

"It changes all the time," Simon says, and wraps the cuff around his arm. His veins stick out more than usual. The running is making him thin, gaunt in the shoulders.

"Of course," Stew says. "Every time you move, it's got to change. Your blood's all over your body. It's just like a cup of water—if you bump it, it sloshes."

June stares at him. She can't tell if he's joking or not. His face is flat, unreadable. She'll have to ask him later.

"Interesting," Simon says, pumping the bulb. "That's quite a theory. It could make you nervous, thinking of yourself about to tip over. But I like it. I like it."

"The body's an ever-changing thing." Stew sounds serious, but he's pulled his mouth tight and long. He's trying not to laugh.

Simon doesn't notice. "It is," he says, "and that's why it's so important to monitor it. So you can anticipate things."

June has to smile. This explains the essence of her father: if you watch something, study it long enough, you will understand and even control it. She thinks of B. F. Skinner doing experiments on his little child, studies of environment and behavior. What good is it to know one's blood pressure or heart rate or degree of wellness every day? The increments of change are minute. They can't be controlled. She could be getting a cavity right this minute, but as long as she doesn't feel any pain, she's probably okay. Stew's cholesterol might be creeping higher, but he won't know until it reaches a certain point.

"You can't anticipate everything," she says.

"Of course not, June." Simon's eyebrows rise. "Nobody said that."

"I didn't say they did." This is one of her father's favorite debating techniques. He argues against things she's never said, hears things she isn't implying, and by the end she's not quite sure what the point of contention was.

"I'm just staying in touch with my body," Simon says. "I'm watching out for anything unusual."

"But taking your pressure once tells you the same thing as taking it ten times." She stops. Her father has folded his hands in his lap. He's frowning. It's best to drop it.

"What will you think about while you're running your marathon?" Stew asks.

Simon brushes some wispy hairs across his bald spot. "What do you mean? I'll be racing."

Stew sits forward in his chair, and June notices a little roll of fat on his belly she hasn't seen before. He's gaining weight in the way skinny people do, getting solid in the middle but keeping his gangly limbs. "Aren't there certain things you'll concentrate on? Chants or encouraging sayings?"

Simon looks blank. He doesn't understand, but he's trying to be polite. June is glad for that, at least.

Stew tries to explain. "Like when I'm out mowing the lawn, and it's the middle of summer, and I'm sweating and sweating. All I want to do is go inside and get a big glass of water, but I've got at least two hours to go. And when I finally—"

"Oh, please, our lawn isn't that big," June says. She can't help correcting Stew, even though she wants to hear what her father could be thinking about. They get ten dollars a month off their rent if they cut the lawn, which is tiny, only meant to suggest the idea of a yard. "It only takes about thirty minutes to do the whole thing."

He tilts his head. "Yeah, but it seems like two hours. That's the point. What do you think about to get you to the end?"

"I'd think about how time passes," June says, "the way it always does, and how, no matter what, I'll eventually be done. And I'd imagine myself in the house drinking the water."

"Wrong," Simon says. "It won't sustain you for twenty-six miles."

"I'm only mowing the lawn."

"But be theoretical. I'm going to be in a lot more pain than you are just pushing a lawn mower. What should I think about?"

Stew smiles. He glances at June, and she rolls her eyes. It's the kind of discussion her father loves, but now they'll be here all night. There's a fine line between a flowing conversation and one that won't end. It's half past nine, and they have to work tomorrow. Stew gets up before it's light to work at the laundry bag factory. And she has to do invoices; it's the end of February, and sales have been high because of Valentine's Day. She'll never be able to give flowers as presents again after seeing how much the shop marks up the roses. Even common gestures of love come at a price.

"I could learn meditation," Simon says, "but I've only got nine months—I don't think you can master it in such a short time, do you?"

June shrugs. "Depends."

"On what?" Stew asks.

"What kind of meditation you're learning, how you apply yourself," June says. "You know. You always read that it takes a lifetime to master."

A lifetime is too long. Her father hates to wait; he wants instant results from his quests. The evidence drags behind him, the gardens tilled but not planted, the electronics workshop with all the unassembled parts, the deluxe chemistry set with the twenty-year-old chemicals still untouched. Disco lessons and art classes, pottery and Mexican cooking, all only started.

Simon looks at Stew. "What else do you suggest? June tells me you ran cross-country in high school."

Stew shifts in his seat. "That was years ago. It was just for fun."

June imagines him pumping his arms and stretching his legs to cover as much ground as possible. He told her once that he was the slowest on the team and ran most of the races alone. The opponents and his teammates pulled so far ahead he couldn't see them.

There is a sudden hissing noise, and she jumps. But it's only her father releasing the blood pressure gauge. "Sorry," he says. "I forgot I was taking my pressure for a second there. Didn't mean to scare you."

"I don't think I was aware of pain," Stew continues. "I mean, I don't think I thought about it. I was only trying to finish."

"I see," Simon says. "I see." He rubs his arm, which is red from the cuff. "My arm feels kind of numb. I wonder how long I left that thing on."

"But you know," Stew says, "it really is a wonderful team sport, cross-country is. Great guys. I knew I was awful, but no one ever teased me about it."

"It really is numb." Simon is moving his arm in a big circle, as if he's doing the one-armed backstroke.

"Keep moving," June says. "I'm sure it's not serious. I bet it's the same as your arm falling asleep."

Stew nods his head. "Just artificially induced, that's all."

"Gee, I don't know."

Stew points to his wrist and looks at June. He's asking what time it is, but she doesn't want to tell him, not while her father is so worried—it'll look bad. He points to his wrist again, his index finger jabbing furiously. Anyone could see it.

"It's about a quarter to ten," Simon says. He has stopped swinging his arm. "Do you have to be home?"

June looks at her fingernails, embarrassed.

Stew clears his throat. "Um, no. No. Actually, I was just wondering."

"Just wondering. I do that sometimes, too."

June tries to smile. "Stew has to go to work early. He has to be there at seven. The sun's not even up yet."

"Yes," Simon says. "That's hard."

They all nod in agreement, and the room is quiet. June can hear the refrigerator humming out in the kitchen, the sound of cars passing the house.

Simon hangs his arm over the side of the couch. Every few seconds, he shakes it and wiggles his fingers.

"Getting better?" June asks.

He shakes his arm harder. "It'll have to, won't it?"

"Well, of course. But if it isn't better, we should do something."

Simon ignores this. He nods to Stew. "How's your work?"

Stew hates the factory. He never talks about it. He's been there for two years and June's still not sure what he does. Something to do with explaining benefits to employees. He calls himself a translator, putting the policies in plain English so the workers won't get ripped off.

Stew gives his fake smile, big in the mouth and not at all around the eyes. "Fine. The same," he says.

"What is it you do again?"

"Insurance stuff. Nothing special."

"It pays the bills," June says. "Just temporary, until something better comes along." Stew is going to be a photographer, that's what he really is. He doesn't make a living at it, but that's his true identity.

Stew glares at her. He must think she's making an apology. It sounds weak, he's told her before. He says either you do your art or you don't; no excuses. Obstacles must be overcome. Otherwise, it's just bad attitude.

"What do you do all day?" Simon looks at Stew, waiting. He can sniff out misery, then prove he's the one who's suffered the most.

"Oh, well, I talk to people about their illnesses and how to file their claims."

"They can't do that themselves?"

"The policies are really hard to read. And I do other stuff, too."

"They love him," June says. "They bake him cakes all the time, and they're always writing him these long letters thanking him." It's true, he brings home a cake about once a week—red velvet, caramel pecan, German chocolate. By the time June and Stew have made a dent in one, another has arrived. They pile up on the kitchen counter, and June throws them out when the stack gets too high.

Simon picks at a hair on his forearm. It's white and longer than the rest. "I've had lots of jobs I hated. Lots."

"Oh yeah?" Stew says. "Which ones did you hate?"

"Just about all of them. The bosses were always bastards. I need to be my own boss." Simon pauses a second and says in a low voice, "But I used to make up love songs to pass the time."

"Love songs?" June can't imagine her father making up songs. He has the most pedestrian taste in music; he's followed the top forty and easy listening stations since she was a teenager. He likes sentiment, fluff, songs with surprise endings. She doesn't think of him as someone with musical ability.

"Yeah. You know, proclamations of desire, lots of pining away, that sort of thing."

"Where are they now?" Stew says.

Simon points to his head. "In here."

"You didn't write them down?"

"Nope."

"Why not?" June says. "I mean, this is really important, like poetry or art or something. You can't just store it in your head." She doesn't see how he can keep a running log, with daily mileage, heart rate, blood pressure, with numerous charts and discussions of hills and pacing, and not write down a single song.

"I thought I'd remember them." Simon smiles. "I mean, I sang them over and over again, through all those jobs. I sang while I drove the elementary school bus and when I was teaching freshman trig at Alamo College. I never thought I'd forget them."

"You forgot all of them?" Stew doesn't believe it either.

"Just about. But that's what I did to pass the time. What do you do?"

Stew is silent, considering.

"Sing me just one line," June says.

"I can't." Simon spreads his hands, palms up. "I really did forget them all. But they were funny. And sad. I could just about make myself weep."

"They were really moving, huh?"

Simon nods.

"I don't do anything to pass the time," Stew says. "I just wait the day out."

Right now, June doesn't care what Stew does. She can imagine her father after work, singing to her mother in the kitchen. Maybe he only sang when they were alone, when nobody else was listening. Her mother would be chopping onions or carrots for some kind of soup, and he would croon earnestly from the table, his hands wrapped around a coffee cup.

"Who did you want to hear you?" she asks now.

Simon's eyebrows rise. "Why, everyone, of course. Everyone who was listening."

"So you were hoping for greatness," Stew says.

"No, I just wanted to be heard."

This is familiar. June's whole life, it seems, this has been her father's greatest complaint: Nobody hears me. It was his response to minor arguments about where to eat out and his missing socks, and to larger events like his divorce. When June was young, she'd try to concentrate on his every word, his tiniest breath. She watched his face, his hands, the way he held his arms, for signs. What was it she should hear? She still doesn't know.

71

"Just one line. Make one up." June doesn't care that she's begging.

"I have to think," Simon says.

He jiggles his legs, reaches for the blood pressure gauge and begins pumping the bulb. It makes small whooshing noises each time he squeezes it. June will have to wait. He takes a long time to answer questions sometimes. She'll think he's forgotten, and just as she's about to ask again, he'll start to speak. Now he looks around the room. His eyes wander from object to object: the rocking chair he bought with her mother at a folk festival; the candlesticks he carved when he decided to teach himself woodworking, before he found out how many years it would take; his running shoes, side by side near the door.

"Boy, it's really hard to come up with a good one," Simon says, finally. "I don't know if I can do it. I had so many, and now I can only remember snippets."

June looks over at Stew. His head weaves a little, and he's having a hard time keeping his eyes open. She watches them close and jerk open a few seconds later. How can he be sleepy? Her father is about to sing.

A loud beeping noise cuts the air, like an alarm clock going off. Everyone jumps. It's coming from the coffee table.

"What, what is it?" Stew looks around the room wildly, caught off guard in his near nap.

Simon slaps his forehead. "Oh, God, I'm sorry." He grabs the blood pressure gauge and fiddles with some knobs on the front. The beeping stops.

"What's wrong?" June says. Maybe it's broken.

Simon shakes his head. "I guess I forgot to turn it off."

Stew rubs his eyes.

"The gauge. It's been on this whole time. It was taking a reading."

"You mean you can take a reading of nothing?" June says.

"I guess so, if you pump it up enough," Simon says.

"There's no reason for them to design it like that," June says.

"They who?" Stew says.

June glares at him. "The scientists, the engineers, or whoever designed this thing."

Simon coughs. "Look, it doesn't matter. There's nothing wrong with the machine. It's my mistake, mine."

Stew smiles. "Don't apologize."

"Such a complicated machine, though," Simon starts to explain. "So smart, it's stupid. When I bought it—"

June cuts him off. "Weren't you going to sing for us?"

"Oh yeah, yeah. I was thinking of something, wasn't I?"

June nods. She doesn't want to interrupt her father's train of thought again. He's on the verge of remembering a line. Maybe her mother was the only one to hear these songs. She certainly hummed a lot of tunes June had never heard elsewhere. June used to try to hum along, but she never knew where the next notes would be. What are you singing, she'd say, but her mother would only answer, I'm just humming, it's not really a song.

June looks at Stew to make sure he's not about to say anything that will lead Simon astray. But he's slumped over, about to fall asleep again.

"Okay, I got it," Simon says. He starts to sing. "My belly is hungry for you, my great big dish of love."

He sings louder. His voice is off tune and a little hoarse. "Smack my lips, grind my teeth, it's you I'm thinking of."

June laughs. "Great, great." He doesn't sound so terrible, a little like a blues singer if she stretches her imagination. It's not inconceivable that he could write songs.

He hangs his head, embarrassed maybe. "It's supposed to be sort of sexy, a declaration of love."

"And who did you love?" she says. At last she'll have the evidence she needs, proof that her parents shared something, some kind of good. Maybe her father tried, and maybe the saying is true: It's the thought that counts.

"Well, the songs were just sort of abstract, really."

"Did you make them up for Mom?" It could be a secret between her parents still. How does it sound, her father might have said. Her mother would nod her small head. Good, she'd say, good. She'd smile her narrow smile and nod some more.

Simon's face wrinkles for a second. He's puzzled by the question. "I don't think so. She was never a good audience."

"What do you mean?" He's got to be lying. "I bet she would have loved it."

"Your mother wouldn't have known how to appreciate it. Like

with everything I did." Simon is squinting his eyes as if he's looking at something far away. "No, I don't think I was singing my songs for anyone in particular."

"Oh." June's throat is tight. She's surprised at how disappointed she feels. She takes a deep breath and looks around the room, packed with furniture and pictures from the house she grew up in. The past she wishes for belongs to no one, a myth no matter how hard she imagines it. She tries to focus her eyes on the wall across from her, but then she sees Stew yawn and stretch his arms over his head.

"I could see that on top forty," he says.

"What good is a love song if it's for no one in particular? Answer me that," June says. She tries her best to sound civil.

"It's just a way to move time along." Simon waves his hand across his face as if he's swatting at something. He turns from her and says to Stew, "So you really think I could be on the radio?"

"Oh, sure." Stew nods his head, then yawns again.

"But it makes you tired, right?"

"No, it wakes me up. I swear."

Simon has folded his arms across his chest, planted both feet on the floor. He isn't going to talk anymore about the singing. It's just an aside to him. A funny thing he used to do. Topic closed, he won't budge. The room is quiet. Simon dips his head and grins, and Stew smiles back. Stew thinks it's funny too, a good story, nothing more. They're on the same side. The way Stew's eyes hang heavy, the way his little belly rolls out make June furious all of a sudden. She can't stand the sight of him.

Her mother and father recede, growing smaller and smaller until they're a speck at the end of a long hallway. If her father made an effort, if he sang to her mother, June isn't going to hear about it. All that passion gone to waste. She thinks of her own possibly rotting teeth, her tedious job, the clear sinking of her life into disappointment, miles of possibility unfulfilled. At the flower shop, the invoices pile up forever, the smell of stale hamburgers and pizza, days and days of hurried lunches. Your plans could flutter away and you wouldn't even notice. Gone, and you hadn't achieved a single one.

"Rude," she says.

"What?" Simon looks over, startled.

"I said, he was rude to fall asleep like that, when you were singing."

"I didn't fall—" Stew uncrosses his legs and sits up straight. "You don't mean that. I know you don't. I've got to work so early."

June nods her head. "You'll sleep your life away. You never notice anything."

"Now, June," Simon says. "Now really."

"I bet your dad wasn't offended," Stew says, and glances at Simon for agreement. Sly, as if he's just trying to calm her down, anything, anything.

"Not a bit," Simon says.

"But I was." She is. It all offends her—blood pressure and songs, unfinished projects. Her father won't run that race. By November he'll be doing something new, tai chi or aerobics, ornithology, French lessons. He'll be just as focused, just as convinced he'll master that thing, too. What makes him so sure he'll finish a marathon when he's never completed anything else?

And Stew won't find time to do his photography, not enough, anyway. He'll keep setting aside money for darkroom equipment, scanning the classifieds for used enlargers. Every month he'll discover he hasn't saved quite enough. She can see it. They'll always be broke. She'll be eating factory cake for years to come, her teeth grainy with sugar, her mind dulled from lack of direction.

Stew glances at her and looks away.

Fine, let him be disgusted. Maybe she's out of line, whatever that means. It doesn't matter. She feels like it. She likes it. She wants to smash something, maybe the blood pressure gauge. Piece of junk. It tells you how your blood's doing, but it doesn't change it. Just like holding a mirror up to your face. So what. You see what you see.

"Sorry," Stew says. "Sorry."

"You didn't know I thought I'd be a singer, did you?" Her father smiles.

"No," she says. She crosses her arms and glares at Stew.

"June, are you okay?" Simon is staring at her. He's got that concerned look.

"Yeah, I'm fine." She looks again at the poster above the couch, of her father racing at top speed toward something. He pays attention to all of his dreams. They arrive, and he listens. Simon, the visionary of whimsy.

"We should go," Stew says, and stands up.

June looks at him leaning above her. His face is drawn, he's hurt. She stands up, too. "Yes," she says, and sighs.

This is what it's like, she thinks, to feel old and a little beaten down. Anything can make you angry, you're mad at it all but there's nothing to do. She wants to go home and rest. She's tired. Simon makes her tired. Stew, trying so hard to smooth everyone out, makes her tired. She'll sleep for a long time, and when she wakes up, they'll still be in the same old life, wishing for better. The present will devour the future, and quietly too.

Boys

At my house there aren't any family board games. We don't sit around the kitchen table eating a bowl of popcorn, rolling the dice, moving our little pieces. It's nothing like TV. At my house you could visit and never hear a thing, hardly any conversation; you could spy for days and we'd never incriminate ourselves.

———

I could do it in my sleep, the act that captures each and every one. It is never the same, and they are always different. They only come to this house once—that's all, just one visit. The boy today is Jere; he has rancid breath and thinks he's irresistible. He stands with his hands in his pockets, stares at the ground, nervous, obviously self-conscious as can be.

I bring him into the house, let him sit on the sofa. He rubs his hands on his knees, leans forward.

"This is my parents' house," I say.

"Of course." His voice squeaks. He wears our high school letter jacket, purple with a gold B on the right side.

"You play sports," I say.

"Yeah, basketball. Coach is really working us this week."

"Mmm. And are you loyal?"

He rubs the back of his neck, raises his eyebrows. "Loyal?"

"Yeah." I pull out the remote control and begin flicking the television on and off. "You know, committed. A loyal member of the Buxton High basketball team, champs of South Texas."

"I guess."

I flick the television to the nature channel. What looks like two lizards mate on a tree branch, their astro-green bodies swaying slightly. The voice-over talks about how chameleons are a dying breed, nearly nonexistent in some countries. "I love lizards," I say. I move my hands gracefully, in an artful way, the pinkie raised delicately. "They're so intriguing."

"They look kind of slimy."

I pretend to be shocked. "Jere. Such talk, and from a member of the basketball team."

"Well, it's true."

Now I've made him defensive. It is time to begin. I make a big deal of closing the drapes to the afternoon sun, of locking the front door. I take my time turning to face Jere.

"Why are you here?"

Jere picks up my mother's glass swan, tinted blue, its long thin neck arching. He moves it along the end table, holding it by the tail and turning it left and right. "Cal told me to visit."

"Cal told you."

"Uh huh."

I sit down again, lean back in my chair, cross my legs. I feel mean today. "Well, it's nothing personal, really, but I don't like you. I don't feel like seeing you."

Jere looks startled. His long face grows longer, whitens. He swallows. "But I thought—" he begins.

"Don't bother," I say. "I really don't feel like it."

I move to open the front door. "I'll see you out," I say, and I watch his gangly body make its way down the walk, the arms swinging, the feet clumsy in their high-tops. The afternoon air is crisp and clear, October days, leaves piling up in the yard.

The boys come up to our house and I let them in. They have smooth necks, finely shaped hands, no sense of humor. Hopeful looks on their faces, arms at their sides. I see them standing on the front step when I peer through the peephole. They stand and wait, surrounded by my mother's potted plants, her azaleas, mouse-ears, aloe vera, spider plants. The boys with cowlicks have wetted them down, the ones without have brushed their hair in a fancy way, forward and into their eyes, enigmatic, or behind their ears, rebellious.

I can tell by their hair how our time will pass. I can tell, also, whether they are in earnest, or whether they have heard about me from other boys. Gossip about things I have done, will do; I am like a dragon queen, mysterious, exotic, not like other girls. None of them true, these stories, but I never bother to set them right.

Yes, I say, what is it. I keep my voice casual, as if I could be any girl, any one at all; they could be lost, in the wrong neighborhood, on someone else's doorstep. They know nothing but my voice, can see only the front door, my mother's seasonal wreaths: corn husks for autumn, pinecones for winter, and eucalyptus in the spring and summer. But these boys don't know I have a mother who changes the wreath every so often, who goes to church, makes the beds, does crossword puzzles, reads all the time.

On the other side of the door, they look small and far away, at the end of a long tunnel, their features rounded at the edges to fit the shape of the peephole. Some shuffle their feet and look away, some stare expectantly at the door. But when I say, Yes, what is it, they invariably answer, I'm here to see Mal. That's my name, Mal, short for Mallory, or, as my father used to say when I was much younger, short for mallard duck. I put my hand on the doorknob and turn the lock. I open the door and there they always are, solitary and real as life.

My father raises earthworms and thinks he's a garden man. My mother works as a computer programmer, punching in binary numbers and special combinations of letters to create the instructions for a hunk of metal. They come home in the early evenings, my father from his uniform store, my mother from her company, and go their separate ways. My father puts on his brand-new pair of jeans and rolls them to his knees. He puts on his sneakers and is gone, hoe in hand, to check on tomato worms and potato bugs, to coax his plants out of the ground. My mother reads biographies, anyone's, as long as they are long and sprawling, detailed, myopic. Not now, she says, I'm reading. About Jane Austen, the Wright brothers, George Washington, Patty Hearst, Lassie the dog. And she means it. You could talk yourself hoarse and she still wouldn't hear.

I go to school, come home, go to school, come home. I try on costumes in my room, put on my grandmother's glass jewelry. I pose on the bed in front of the mirror, watch myself act like someone much older, more alluring. I speak in a husky voice, talk to the mirror. It's me again, I say, I'm here to watch. I let out a low giggle and exchange knowing glances with my reflection. How lovely you are, I think, when you look like someone else.

My friend Jena is scared of boys; they worry her. I'm never getting married, she says. I try to explain that she would be marrying a man, perhaps with a deep voice and rough skin.

"No," she says, "it doesn't appeal to me." We are walking to school, poking our sticks into cracks in the sidewalk and pulling them out, carrying them by our sides.

"Everyone does it." I point my stick toward the sky. "Besides, you don't have to like them to marry them."

"Sure you do," Jena says.

"Lots of people do it just to do it."

"Not me."

"I don't see what's so wrong with it." And I don't, not really. In the Middle Ages people married for the sake of convenience, survival, nothing fancy, no romance. My parents don't appear particularly in love, but they hardly ever fight. Their garden, their books, they seem okay.

Jena gives my arm a light shove. "You like boys more than is normal," she says. "You like them the way some people like their pets or their televisions." She thumps her book bag against the side of her leg. "You like to watch them and trick them."

"I'm doing an experiment."

"How?"

"I'm testing the range of their nature, seeing what they'll do. I need to know their reaction to every possible situation. Boys are dangerous."

"It's because you've never really gone out with one."

"And you," I say, turning to give Jena my most sarcastic smile, "have only gone out with one. Look where it got you."

"We'll miss the bus—we've got to walk faster."

"It got you nowhere. You were depressed for weeks when Jack, as in 'Hi, I'm God, I mean Jack,' dumped you. I'm just trying to prepare."

We're at the bus stop now, the only kids in ninth grade who still have to ride it, who don't have cars or parents who are willing to drive us. Lucas Schneider, a shrimpy eighth grader, is handing out cigarettes he stole from his father's top dresser drawer. "Right behind the underwear," he says.

Jena points at him. "See, he'll always lie until the day he dies. He's doing it now. He'd be terrible to date, to marry. Especially with those teeth—they're so crooked."

I nod. "Yeah, bad teeth, bad character."

She shrugs. "You can always tell."

"You'd be so much more attractive if you'd pull your hair back," my mother tells me. We're in the kitchen, slicing onions and celery for the vegetable soup. A tear rolls down my mother's face, from the onions I know, but she would have me think otherwise.

"Need a paper towel, Mom?" I tear one off the roll and hand it to her.

"It pains me to see you ignoring your potential. You have the profile of H. D., but no one can see it."

"Who's that?"

"A famous woman poet with a very nice jawline." My mother pours olive oil into a skillet and turns on the burner. "You could look like her."

"Pull my hair back how?"

"In a ponytail or with barrettes."

I stick a piece of celery in my mouth. "Only nice girls do that."

"But Mal—"

The sound of the front door opening distracts her, my father home from work. Every afternoon he slips in, quiet as can be. He heads straight for the bedroom, for his gardening pants, his work shirt. October days shorten, and he races with the fading light for time in the garden. And every afternoon, my mother tries to intercept him, to ask him questions.

"How was work?" she says now. She rolls her eyes at me, as if we share some conspiracy. "He never wants to tell," she mutters.

"Fine," my father calls out. He clomps up the back stairs, his footsteps shaking the whole house, gigantic, monstrous.

My mother stirs the onions, and their pungent odor rises into the air. I hand her the cutting board with all the celery on it; she slides the pieces in. They sizzle and pop.

"Can't even spend two seconds to say hello," she says, shaking her head. "Can't spend time away from those precious vegetables."

I nod slightly, not wanting to agree too much with either side.

———————

Next day's boy is fat and mild. My mother works late and my father eats dinner out with his best friend. The house is mine. I rush from room to room, trying to create the right ambience. I put the chairs back to back, away from the television, away from each other, so that anyone sitting in them can see only the wall, the doorways, no people. I drape my mother's scarves over the lamp shades, and the light seeps through in hues of blue and red, soft orange, green. I place a few peanuts in saucers and put each saucer next to a chair, little snacks. This boy, Jeffrey Weems, called earlier to make an "appointment," he said. He prided himself on his cleverness, such a euphemism. I could tell. But that's what he asked for, and that's what he will get.

I rummage through my mother's closet, searching for the perfect outfit. Not the blue party dress, not the burnt brown pantsuit with zippers up the sides, the beige skirts she usually wears, the muted tones, stylish on a woman her age. I am nearly to the end of the rod when I find it—her black dress-up suit, made from thick, scratchy material. Tapered at the waist, padded shoulders, hip-hugging skirt, the slit up the back. I grab her red silk shirt to match. I slip off my clothes, fasten the skirt around my waist. I look in the mirror: a little big at the waist, perhaps, a bit baggy in the hips, but no matter. A safety pin or two will do the trick. How lovely you are, I say to my reflection, such a nice outfit. A doctor might wear such a thing, one in the peak of her medical career, at the height of fashion. So tell me, Jeffrey, I say to the mirror in my lowest, sternest voice, what is it that brings you here? Who are your references?

I wander into the living room, begin the wait. I sit on the floor in front of the television, click it on with the remote. I cross my legs, careful not to wrinkle the skirt, and watch some cartoon character drinking from a vat of boiling liquid. I can't tell if it's supposed to be funny or dramatic or what. It's not a cartoon I usually watch. I wonder if Jeffrey will be any fun; I've never really talked to him. He's in my math class, but he always sits in the back with all the tall guys, hunched over his geometry book. He's neither loud nor quiet, as far as I can tell, just a run-of-the-mill boy, his T-shirts and big sneakers and blue jeans. When the doorbell rings, the news is just beginning. I've been waiting almost an hour.

I open the door and in my deepest, coldest voice say, "You're late."

He laughs, not at all worried. "I'm late everywhere."

"That doesn't make it okay." I fold my arms across my chest. "We had an appointment."

He shrugs. "Call it what you will." He has curly hair and a full face, his belly hanging over his jeans, not the kind of fat that repulses me, but football fat, big-boned fat. His hands are large but not fleshy, the fingers somehow feminine, tapering, on such a solid frame.

"Come in and have a seat," I say, gesturing past the doorway. "You're late, and my mother comes home at six thirty, so we don't have much time."

———————

I wish, once in a while, for a brother and sister. I wish we had a pet. Anything to break up the silences that last into the evenings, my mother curled up in the couch with her life stories, my father counting out zinnia seeds on the kitchen table. I am the go-between, the only one who gets spoken to, strictly in instructional commands: Go tell your father I need to borrow his car tomorrow; mine's in the shop. Tell your mom I'm using it to help Freddy move a sofa out of his apartment. Ask your father to put some water on to boil, since he's in there anyway. Does your mom want her usual cream and a pinch of sugar? Tell him yes.

I know I'm digging a little trench between the living room and the kitchen, all this walking back and forth; already the carpet is faded, threadbare. One day they'll both look up at the same time, glance around the room. Where's Mal, they'll ask in unison, but I'll be under the earth by then, trudging my ten-foot path to the other side.

I'll burrow through caves and rivers of thick mud, through the cores of dormant volcanoes. I'll be invincible, digging my path away from here.

"So, what do we do?" Jeffrey asks. "What is it that all these guys rave about?"

I shrug, adjust my jacket, which is sliding off my left shoulder. "Depends. Different things."

His eyes widen. He has folded his hands in his lap, attentive. "Oh yeah? Do I get to choose?"

"No. I do." I nod toward the sofa. "Lie down."

He stretches himself out on the sofa, and it sags a little in the middle. His legs are too long; he has to dangle his feet over the armrest.

"Now. Tell me about your childhood." I rap a pencil against the palm of my hand. I wish I had glasses so I could push them up the bridge of my nose. How intelligent I would appear.

"Why?"

"Tell me. You're paying by the hour."

"No one said anything about money," he says, sitting up abruptly.

"Like any appointment, this costs money."

"But it isn't real. You aren't qualified to do anything."

I can see why he gets A's on his geometry tests. Such logic. I smile. "Then why are you here?" I say, and seat myself in a chair across the room, facing the hallway.

"Who designed this living room anyway?" he says. "It looks like hell. It looks like a house for people who can't stand each other."

I nod, but of course he can't see me. The way I've arranged the furniture, no one has to look at anyone else, no one has to talk.

He begins again. "I said—"

"I heard you. Yes, you're right. That's how it is in this house—no one is allowed to talk with anyone once they enter. House rules." I smile at the hallway, dark and shadowed. "But of course, since my parents aren't home, we'll make an exception. Talk away."

Jeffrey is silent. We sit there in the early evening, the sun setting behind the house, and say nothing. I tap the pencil against my knee, and Jeffrey sounds as if he is chewing his fingernails, an odd gnawing sound, like a large rat would make.

Finally, I stand, stretch my arms over my head. "Well," I say, "time to go. Thank you for coming."

Jeffrey gets up too, stuffs his hands in his pockets. "You know, this is really stupid," he says. "I can't believe I let myself get caught in this." He shakes his head.

"See you." I show him out the door.

"What a hoax," he mumbles, already halfway down the steps. "What a friggin' hoax."

How must it feel, I wonder, to have a boy wiggling around inside you? What do you think about? How long does it last? The minute you do it, are you in love? Where do you look? Do you look the boy in the face, or do you look at the ceiling, or the blankets, or what? Maybe you close your eyes so it's less embarrassing. And what do you do with your hands? How do you keep from wondering if you look dumb, like a frog on its back in the road? It's these things that bother me, the questions I cannot ask a real person. They rattle around in my head at the wrong time, when I'm eating supper at our silent table, or in the middle of an English exam, or in the school cafeteria while everyone eats their corny dogs as if it's a completely normal thing.

I follow my father around in the garden as he weeds and waters, gathers the last of the tomatoes. "Watch out you don't step on any of the carrots. They look kind of like weeds."

"I know, I know," I mumble. My father has divided his little plot of land—the size of a large bathroom—into rigid rows, perfectly straight, exactly a foot between each. How can he walk through here every day and never take a wrong step? It seems miraculous, especially since he is not a dainty man, no grace; his motions are always awkward, jerky.

"Your mother wants to know why you rearranged the furniture like that last week." He seems nervous, and I know she has made him promise he will ask. Up to now, neither has questioned me about it.

I stare at the bug bites in the spinach leaves. "You've got insect problems," I say, and point to a gaping hole.

My father bends down to inspect the damage. "Poor baby," he

whispers, caressing a particularly mottled leaf, and I am surprised to hear it.

"It was a game," I say. "Jena and I were playing a game."

"You're too old for that."

"Huh?" How would he know what I was old enough for?

"It just doesn't seem like something you would do." He shakes his head, reaches over and picks a tomato, turns it around in his hand. "It seemed unusual to us."

"I'm still normal as can be," I say. "It was just a game, and I forgot to move the chairs back."

"What kind?"

"Of game?"

"Yes."

"Oh, well, we were pretending we lived in a futuristic society, and it was socially unacceptable to face other people in a living room setting."

He nods. "Some kind of science project."

"Yeah." And, I tell myself, that's not much of a lie at all.

I pass my parents' bedroom on my way to brush my teeth that night, and I see it: the truth of their marriage. There's my mother, crying into the bedspread. She's got her hands cupped over her face like she's worried her eyes will fall out, only she's making little sobbing sounds. The reading lamp is on, and she's surrounded by jagged shadows in the shape of cacti, mesquite trees, saguaro: a desert setting. They leap out all around her. I pause and start to ask if she's all right, but then I don't. She might hate me later for finding her out, for knowing her secrets.

In the bathroom I squeeze paste on my toothbrush and concentrate on moving the brush up and down, top row, bottom row, back, front. I tell myself she could be crying about anything: a bad day at work; a particularly moving section of her latest book, a thick one about Hans Christian Andersen; or maybe the fact that I forgot to put the furniture back. She spent a whole evening last week moving the chairs to their old positions, scolding me the whole time, but she wouldn't let me help. "You did it out of spite," she said. "You'll probably put them back the wrong way, too."

A bit of toothpaste drops from my brush, and I turn the faucet on to wash it down the drain. It's none of these things, though. Even I can figure that out. I know my father's still outside, hoeing in the dark, expanding his garden to the size of our kitchen, turning the dirt over so it can breathe. He and the moon out there in the crisp air. He's talking to the spinach, guarding against tomato worms, his babies the lettuce, his babies the carrots, all of them.

When Jena calls on the phone I am staring at my feet. I have just discovered two big lumps, one on each foot, on the outside where the littlest toes join the sole. I wonder how big they will get, how long they've been there.

"I've got bunions, I think," I say. "They're huge and hard, like bones."

"I thought only old ladies got those, or fat ladies, or something," Jena says. She doesn't sound worried. "What do you care? You aren't a foot model."

"No," I say, "but my mother's friend had to have one removed, and it was really painful. She couldn't walk for weeks."

Jena laughs. "How was your date?"

"You mean my appointment? With Jeffrey Cow?"

"He's not that fat."

I bet he has bunions. "No, it was fine." I tell her about the couch, the chairs, how good I looked in my mother's slit skirt. Of course, he couldn't see me most of the time, but still. I tell her about him gnawing his fingernails.

"Wow," Jena says. "Nobody's stomach can digest that."

"Yeah. It's true, nobody's can. And then he left."

"That's all?"

"Of course. You know that, Jena." We never do anything, these boys and I, but they're too embarrassed to tell each other. They keep showing up, leaving disappointed. "It's like the emperor's new clothes, except nobody gets naked," I say.

"Uh huh. Aren't you literary tonight."

"With bunions." I touch one of the lumps again. "I guess it's because none of my shoes have ever fit."

After we hang up, I hear my father coming down the hall, finished at last with his plants. My mother has been in bed for hours now. I'm supposed to be in bed, too. I lie down quick and hope he'll think I accidentally left the light on. I lie as still as I can, breathing what I imagine are normal, shallow sleep breaths. I hope my eyelids aren't fluttering. I try not to squinch them too hard.

I wait and wait, but he never comes and turns out the light. He walks right past my door, straight on till morning, I guess. My father, absentminded, out of it.

Boys walk tall and carry big sticks. Boys gather in groups, huddle around each other, brushing against each other gruffly. When they look at you, they look past you, maybe trying to find a girl like them, one who looks past them in the same way. So they won't notice how hard it is to connect. Like my parents. Maybe we should have living rooms with opposable furniture. So we could all live together, separately. At least we could acknowledge it. We wouldn't have to pretend so hard.

Charles arrives and I am sitting on the front steps doing the crossword puzzle from that morning's newspaper. I have forgotten he is coming. I am sitting in the last of the warm fall air, watching the leaves take over our yard, wondering if my father will consider this one of his gardening duties, or if he will think it's plain old raking leaves, a job for me. "Hey," Charles says, "what'cha doing?"

I point with my pen at the newspaper. "I'm almost halfway through. You weren't supposed to come today," I lie. "I'm not ready for you. I don't have anything planned."

"Who says you have to plan anything?" Charles squints at me. He always squints, it seems—maybe a bad habit, or maybe he just can't see. Whenever I talk with him, I feel as if he is looking at me from a long distance.

"No one. I like to."

"I wrote the day down when I called," he says. "I know it can't be wrong. Why're you waffling on me?"

"Obviously, you wrote it down wrong." I scramble now, try to seem fierce, the one in control.

He sits next to me on the step. His legs are so long, he looks as if he will eat them, the way his knees are bunched up around his chin, his hands wrapped around his ankles. He smiles. "Something always goes wrong with you, I bet."

"What do you mean?" At first it sounds as if I might have a disease, or some tragic flaw, like we learned in English, that makes me both a hero and an idiot.

"I can tell from the stories." He points to three down on the puzzle. "That's flapjack," he says, "another word for pancake."

I don't say anything. I'm not sure of all the stories people have told about me, what they are.

"They're too wild. Too many good things happen, like the movies or a good peep show."

"What's a peep show?"

"See, if these things were true, you'd know what it is. You'd know it's a dirty movie. In some of the stories I hear, you watch them like they were Shakespeare, quote from them and everything."

My eyes widen. I can't help it. I've never thought of that.

"Yeah, I can tell. You've never done any such thing."

I stare at the ground, at the crack in the cement where the step meets the sidewalk. A line of ants is carrying off the remains of a piece of cracker I left the day before, crumb by little crumb. I can't think what to say. It's true, and I know if I try to cover for it he'll call my bluff. The thing about Charles is he's in all the honors classes, but he's smarter than a lot of the nerdy guys in there. He looks like a boy who forgets to eat, so skinny, but he's a runner on the cross-country team, and it's supposed to make him faster. I was just born this way, he said one day in English class, I had skinny ancestors.

"So," I say, "you don't have any idea what I've done."

"Doesn't matter. You haven't done any of the stories, which means the guys made them up, which means you don't do anything."

A strange thing happens here. He's so smart and he's telling this true thing, about how I am a liar and no good because I never do what I imply, and I look at his lips. They are a little cracked, sort of chapped from running on windy days. They are thin, like he might grow up to be a nervous man. But I can't stop staring at them. I forget all about the ants and their cracker crumbs, and I forget that I have a pen in my left hand.

"Your pen's bleeding all over nine across," he says.

"Oops," I say, and then I feel stupid and giddy, such a useless thing to say. I hate it when my father says this to my mother—he looks silly, caught off guard, as if he will have a lot of explaining to do.

Charles stretches out his legs. They go nearly forever, it seems, with those big clunky running shoes stuck on at the ends. "Well," he says, "what are we going to do?"

I shrug. "I don't know. I'm working on this puzzle right now." I wonder what he looks like when he runs, if he pumps his arms furiously, or leans into the wind, enduring the forces of nature—rain and cold, the sun beating down. I imagine the elongated muscles of his legs, flexing and extending. I wish I could see him run.

"We could go on a walk." Charles stands up, all ready to go.

"Nah," I say. "When's your cross-country practice?"

He nods. "Ah. A sports fan. Tomorrow at two." He brushes a strand of hair from his eyes; he needs a haircut soon, my mother would say. "Come on, Mal. Let's go. It's just a walk. We won't even go very far—around the block maybe."

I imagine myself sitting in the bleachers, watching all the running boys do their warm-up exercises, evenly positioned on the football field. Charles would push his hair out of his eyes and lean to touch his head to his knee, and all around him the runners would do the same thing.

"Well," I say, "all right. But only because I feel like it, not because you asked me to."

He laughs. "Yeah, right, we just happen to both be walking around the same block."

"Yeah," I say, and I hide the crossword puzzle and the pen behind my mother's potted mouse-ears.

———————

We walk past the Breuers' dog, some kind of Alaskan thing, big, with too much hair. It barks, follows us the length of the fence, stands on its hind legs, tall as a man. Charles grabs my arm, and I can feel his grip tighten.

"It's okay," I say. "He can't get out, can't jump worth beans. I guess he weighs too much."

"We had a dog like that once, one that couldn't jump. My mom said she was too lazy."

"We never had any dogs." My father was afraid they'd ruin the garden, dig it up for spite, maybe sleep on top of the lettuce, crush their fragile heads.

"I actually like cats better," Charles says, "because they do things for themselves, not for anyone else."

And soon we are talking about all the pets we ever had: my pet rocks, the goldfish that used to leap out of the tank and land behind our couch, a cat we had that ran away, and Charles's family's lineage of dogs, all of them stupid but nice, the way dogs are. I have to walk fast to keep up with Charles, and we stop at the Bestway to get a soda, pass the can back and forth. He seems pretty normal, normal as Jena, normal like a person should be, carrying on a conversation as if it's easy as breathing. I don't feel like he's watching me, like I have to be a certain way. He talks about the cross-country team, how they're going to run the fastest times ever, how when he runs he thinks only about running. And then I ask him if runners ever get bunions, if it's a common thing, and we walk all over the neighborhood, past the rows of houses leaning forward to hear.

A few days later my parents fight. First time ever. I'm sitting in my bedroom looking at my geometry notes and thinking about my birthday—in a month I will be fifteen—and the voices rise up the stairs like vapors. At first it sounds like the TV is on really loud, but then when I listen I recognize my mother's voice buried in the shrillness, my father's in the bellowing. It jars me in my seat; I sit up straight, trying to catch the words.

"You never talk to me," my mother yells, her voice nearly cracking. "You spend all your time in that garden. I ought to pull up every one of those damn vegetables."

"You never care what I have to say. You read all the time. It's like talking to a stone."

Then there's a mixture of their two voices, softer now, which I can't hear. I think of them in the living room, wonder if they stand facing each other like boxers, or if they sit on the sofa, legs crossed and swinging. I can't picture them either way, and I'm scared to spy.

My father says, "Mal will hear. You better lower your voice."

And my mother surprises me. She says she hopes everyone hears, even the neighbors, they've probably got their ears pressed to the side of the house right now. She hopes their eardrums break from the shock.

"Lower your voice," my father yells, and my mother begins to laugh.

I sit at my desk drawing triangle after triangle, obtuse, acute, right. They pile up on each other but I keep drawing them. The black from my pencil smears all over the paper and the sides of my hands, and I don't care. I try to think of a way to stop them: maybe I should roll down the stairs, pretend I've had a bad fall, or begin to yell myself, up here in my bedroom, a nervous breakdown over geometry postulates. But I sit at my desk, quiet as a mouse, frozen. I think about how, when I am forty, I will have a house of my own, a life I can't even imagine now. Maybe I'll have bundles of children running rampant through the rooms, crusts of bread held tight in their hands. Or I'll have a tent in the mountains; up there all alone, I'll feed the bears peanuts and Tootsie Rolls, and they'll like me best. Or I could be famous, for what, it's hard to say. But these things happen.

This is what I think while my mother begins to cry—the second time in a month—and my father, too. I listen to both of them, down there in the living room sobbing away. My father is loud, uncontained, my mother quieter, those little gasps from before. And I feel myself begin to cry, too, tears landing all over my triangles. A house full of sobbing people, crybabies. I imagine tears rolling down the sides of the walls, trickling in rivulets to my father's garden, down the front path to the street. A phenomenon, certainly; someone should take note. Something to be remembered. The tears will flood my father's plants, ruin the books my mother has stacked so meticulously in the basement. Mildew will set in. The plants will choke and wither, and up here I will draw triangle after triangle long after my parents have gone to bed, long after these first words have been said, and the fight has broken.

Hovercraft

I cannot be contained. Try to keep me good and quiet, agreeable, concise, but you'll find it's to no avail. I say what I say, and you can either take it or leave it.

This is what I tell my children, not really children anymore, grown up and aloof, their long faces cautious and closed, their legs crossed and arms folded tight across their chests. They sit on my couch and nod and murmur, anything to agree, to make the story end sooner, whatever it is I'm telling them. But my stories have ideas and lengths of their own, and it's not right to cut them short, to chop off their hands and feet so they sit paralyzed and lumpy. I take my time, and every detail matters; I believe in the equality of details.

Not that anything's really equal or fair—we all know that. Look at my kids: they resemble their mother, my ex-wife and beloved enemy. They have her narrow moon face and her tiny white teeth, perfect in a row when they smile. And they smile at the wrong times, during the serious parts of what I am talking about. When I make a joke, their faces crease into frowns, and it is like three of my ex-wife sitting there. I could spit and curse, but usually I smile at my own joke because you should always be good to yourself. The theme in all the self-help books is "Mother and father thy own self." And so I go on to the next part of the story. Maybe I slow it down even more, see if I can get their feet to tap out the passing time. One two three, one two three. My three children, mapping waltz steps on my dusty wood floors.

The oldest, June, has a baby named Lila and a husband, too, but I can never remember his name. She could have done better, married someone a little louder, more generous in the heart. Not that he doesn't treat her right. It's me I'm talking about. I caught him rolling his eyes, no mistake, the exaggerated boredom a window into his soul. I was telling the story of how I used to drive a school bus, and I was explaining the mechanics of driving, which is sort of a trick, all the yellow metal and the yawping children, the green vinyl seats, difficult to make a sharp turn with all that. A hunk of metal and squirming bodies taking all roads at a steady thirty-five miles an hour. Most of the knobs and buttons on the dashboard don't actually work, and every school bus is different, so you have to get to know yours well, all the bumps and jolts, the occasional grinding whines special clues to its personality.

I was to the part where I explain about the gearshifts and what they can mean to the bus, and I looked up. There he was, what's-his-name, rolling his eyes. I caught him.

I stopped midsentence and stared. He eventually turned his green eyes that June is so fond of away, examined his fleshy hands, folded them in his lap.

"Is there something you'd like to listen to instead?" I said.

"No, of course not," June's husband said. "Go right ahead."

June leaned forward, watching us both, waiting for something to happen. She wants us to get along, silent and slow, bumping into each other benevolently like the giant carps underwater at the zoo.

My other kids, Martha and Walt, slumped back on the couch. Walt sighed—he sighs a lot, and I've finally decided it's his way of breathing. I try not to take it personally.

"Continue," Martha said, and brushed her thin dark hair from her face. "You were talking about the bus gears."

I glared at June's husband—Stew, I just remembered—and tried to make my voice nonchalant. "I don't want to bore any of the newcomers," I said.

"Don't worry about me." Stew uncrossed his legs and smiled.

Not the same as an apology, though, all we want in life: the rights and wrongs balancing, their weights and sizes equal, canceling each other out.

"But I do worry about you, Stew," I said. "I do."

"No need to, Dad," June said. "That's my job."

They think appeasement will shut me up, smooth me over, but

see how rough I am, how gray and rough. I decided to finish the story, even though it might have been more fun to clam up, make them beg me to finish it, all in the name of hurt feelings and, of course, justice.

June and Stew nestled against each other, and I tried to ignore June's hand on his knee, a kind of betrayal. True, they're married, but what better proof that June was taking the side against mine, the way my children have always done? Trained by their mother from an early age, from the minute they began to breathe the bitter air of the world.

———

June and Walt and Martha. We used to call them in to dinner, in for a bath, in to kiss the visiting relatives good-bye. My wife and I were devoted parents, with the exception that we couldn't stand each other's company. It happened gradually, quietly, a plant growing under the house, turning the soil dull and dry. But still our children came rushing home, news of the day pouring out of their tiny mouths, who got beat up at school, whose gerbil escaped during Show and Tell, whose teacher bent down weeping behind her desk in the middle of science class. They rushed in and filled the frozen air with noise. Their bony bodies smelled of earth and sweat, and they'd lean against me on the couch and slap a book down on my lap. "Read this," they'd say, their voices serious, demanding. "It's about the cat who goes to China with three fish in his mouth." They listened, wiggling a while and then holding still, intent on the cat's travels, riding out into the world on the sound of my voice.

———

Now it was February, and soon they would be over for their monthly visit. A Sunday afternoon, unusually bright for this time of year, not the gray dampness so common in winter. I cleared the newspapers from the table and the floor next to the couch, loaded the dish-washer with the plates and mugs that covered most of the surfaces of furniture. I even refrained from lighting incense—Walt says it feels like he's breathing great quantities of laundry detergent when he has to smell the stuff. I think it gives a room atmosphere, but I wanted everything to go right.

I planned to tell the story of how I learned to channel. More otherworldly and compelling than the school bus, and fresh, because I hadn't told it to anyone yet. It had just happened to me a few weeks before. I signed up for a weekend class taught by a real shaman named Jonas Caribou. The brochure guaranteed that students would have at least one channeling experience by the end of the session.

"Find your soul floating in the air and bring it home," it read. I was in the Crystal and Light Bookstore just a few blocks from my house, and I saw a stack of flyers by the door. I stood there and read, apologizing every two seconds to the customers who filtered in, their faces tense and drawn because of course they hadn't found their souls either. The brochure talked about how most people's souls hover just a few feet above their physical selves, following along quietly as their owners go about their days. Most of us imagine our souls anchored to our hearts, somewhere in the upper chest area. It's a common misconception.

I turned the brochure over and discovered that Jonas Caribou would be in town that weekend. He was charging a lot of money, though, and usually I think of shamans as not needing so much of that kind of thing. Not than I'm against people having to pay for their souls. Folks have been doing it for years. I decided to give it a try, and in the next few days I found myself looking up often, resisting the urge to wave.

———————

Walt and Martha are the closest. Just over a year apart. They look the same, the slivered blue eyes and long limbs, same thin hair, except Walt is beginning to bald. It's okay, you'll survive it, I want to say, you got it from me. But even baldness is passed along the mother's side. It's just coincidence that I lost my hair at the same age. He'll spend most of his twenties under a baseball cap.

Walt and Martha fought each other all the way through their childhood, and when they made it to the other side, they were friends. They go to the movies together, have each other over for dinner, debate the endings of novels, and play Idiot's Delight, Spades, Hearts, and even more complicated card games late into the night.

None of my children will play with me, especially games involving numbers, because I always win. Always have, always will. I have a talent for numbers, well, really a genius for them, and it makes me hell on the game court. Walt declared it years ago, when he was eight, crossed his arms and told me he wouldn't ever play checkers with me again. Martha chimed in. "Yeah," she said in her high girl's voice, "and not anything else, either." Walt sighed and shook his head like an old man, like me now, and stalked outside to play soccer, just him and the ball and some rules he'd made up.

Martha put her hands on her hips and tapped her foot. "See, Dad," she said, "you're too smart for kids. You have to let us win once in a while. It's like sharing."

"Sharing?"

"Yes. The way we learned in school."

"What about the other rule?" I said.

"What rule?" Martha wrapped her coat around her like a cloak.

"The one about not lying ever."

"So?"

"So if you let someone win, isn't it a kind of lie?"

Martha's face clouded with doubt. "Not one that matters," she said.

She already knew that some lies grow out of generosity, kindness even. The proof is in her face all these years later: she might be listening hard, following every turn of the plot, but I'm never sure. A hint of politeness hanging faint in the air, and Martha won't admit it. Indulging me, like the other two.

Martha and Walt sat on easy chairs I'd pulled out for them, and June leaned against Stew on the couch and murmured into his ear. He smiled and nodded, and for a second I thought she must be saying something about me. But then he turned to her and kissed her on the nose. Right here in my house. As if the rest of us were invisible, as if their love is so spectacular we should all see it.

I cleared my throat, but they didn't stop. Walt and Martha played Paper Scissors Rock to my right, absorbed in the game, cursing and jostling each other when they tied.

"Hey," I finally said. They all looked up, startled. "An incredible thing happened to me."

"Oh yeah?" Martha said.

"How about that," Walt said, and repositioned his baseball cap so the bill faced the back.

"I had a life-changing experience a few weeks ago. Truly life-changing," I said. "I learned to channel. I can channel right through to my soul if I want."

June and Stew just nodded their heads and separated, crossing their legs and folding their hands in their laps. Stew coughed once and smiled.

"I'm sure you're wondering just what channeling is," I said.

They looked at me, waiting, their faces unreadable. I began to see that I might encounter more skepticism than I had anticipated. Their mother, the biggest questioner of all, her dubious blood coursing through their veins like warning lights. But I plunged forward.

"I didn't much believe it either at first," I said. "Such a silly sounding word. I haven't looked it up, mind you, but I'm pretty sure its root word is 'to change,' which certainly applies here."

Walt began to tap his foot slowly, tempo of a funeral march, and I knew I was beginning to lose them. I clapped my hands together. "Well," I said, "let's say that it's just like a TV channel, only more spiritual, of course." I paused for a second to let my words sink in.

"Of course," June said.

"You pick up energy from Out There, and, well, you receive it."

"Just like an antenna," Stew said, "a human antenna. Received knowledge."

I glared at him just to be safe. I don't know why I keep inviting him over. "Channeled knowledge," I said, "not received."

"What made you want to learn to channel?" Martha said. "You're usually so, uh, kind of scientific, don't you think?"

"Exactly," I said. "But this is a real science, an art. Rather, an artful science, as all higher callings are."

"Huh," Stew said.

"Oh, yeah." Walt yawned. "Jake, in my dorm—his mother says she's a channeler."

"Really?" I said. Maybe I could meet her.

"Yeah, but she says she's a lot of different things. Like, a queen from the twelfth century, a World War Two fighter pilot, some Egyptian cleric's pet cat. A bunch of things. Jake's told me, but I can't remember them all."

Martha tossed her head. "Quite the past life," she said. "Too bad she's never been a rock or a mosquito, something lower on the food chain."

"She was a cat," Walt said.

"The cat of a cleric," Martha said, "not an ordinary cat."

"Delusions of grandeur," June said.

This was not going well. I had to rein them in. "Listen," I said, "listen. This is really true. With practice you can see your own soul. You can see all its pasts and presents."

They watched me still.

"It's almost always hovering just a few feet above your head."

"What is?" Stew said.

"Your soul, dummy." June gave him a fake punch.

Walt and Martha looked up at the ceiling, checking to see, maybe trying to catch a glimpse, the way I had done that first time in the bookstore.

"Right there." I pointed in the air above them. "You're looking in the right place, but the shaman I met says you find it by searching within first."

"You've been seeing a shaman?" Martha's eyes grew wide.

"Yep." Finally I had their attention. "Want to know what I am?"

"What do you mean 'what you are'?" Stew said.

"The form my soul takes, the way it appears."

"What. What are you?" June leaned forward, her elbows on her knees.

"Guess."

"A knight," she said.

"No."

"An inventor," Martha said.

"Wrong again."

"An autodidact," Stew said.

"Please," I said, "puleeeease."

"Your same old self," Walt guessed.

"Wrong, all of you. Wrong."

June sighed. "Just tell us and be done with it."

"All right," I said. "Okay. Although I can't fathom it myself." I thought about how to present it in the best light possible, but there wasn't much I could do to improve it. "I'm, well, I'm a social, communal animal, one of the very best."

"Yes?" Martha said.

"I'm a penguin, it turns out," I said.

Well, of course they all laughed. They laughed for a long time, about five minutes. I kept saying, "Wait, wait," but it was no use. They were lost. I'd be the story they told at dinner parties and informal gatherings, just the place for a light anecdote about their eccentric father.

"Forget it," I said, and pounded my fist on the coffee table. A juice glass I'd overlooked earlier wobbled and was still. "It's obvious I'm just a caricature to you. I've known it for years."

"That's what's so endearing about you," Walt said, and maybe he was joking, ridiculous in his backwards cap. But I stood up and left the room. Not one of them called for me to come back.

Sometimes June brings the baby Lila over and I get to hold her for a few minutes. Lila is bald except for one thin strand of red hair that June tries to comb to the side. We look alike, not counting the red, which she must have gotten from Stew's family. Lila stares at me and places her perfect hands on my head, and they're cool and damp. She's calm, inquisitive, the way all my children were at that age. Then she might say something, but it's mostly saliva and vowel sounds. I'm never sure what she's getting at.

"Urple," she says, and pats her hands on my head.

"Yes, exactly," I say, and we sit for a while.

June fusses over Lila. She hands her a bland cookie or adjusts her socks, which are always sliding off. Or she offers to hold the baby. But Lila ignores all this, and for a few minutes it is just me and her, my most captive listener, too young and too wise to answer.

At the conference where I discovered I was a penguin, hundreds of men and women wandered around, some quiet and pensive, others anxious, giddy, anticipating the possibility that they might not get to see their souls on the first try. I'm a scientist at heart, so I had the proper dose of skepticism. The hotel lobby was full of people, and I wondered what would happen if all our souls appeared at once, hovering overhead like a bunch of balloons. Think of the chaos.

Finally the doors to the conference room opened, and we rushed in, pushing past each other for the seats closest to the front. I ended up next to a woman named Myra who sat hunched into herself, her hands folded in her lap like she was praying.

"I'm here to get rid of the evil that inhabits my left shoulder blade," she said.

I don't believe in humoring people—I get that all the time from my children—but who wants to argue with that?

"Huh," I said. "Well, good luck."

Before we had a chance to discuss Myra's shoulder further, Jonas Caribou came on stage. The crowd gasped. He was such a little man. We had all expected someone taller, thinner, with less resemblance to a Santa.

"Greetings, all," he said, and he didn't even touch the microphone. His voice was deep, rich, clearly the source of his strength and charisma.

Then he began to sing.

> "Sacred soul, sacred soul, come to me,
> show yourself by the count of three,
> give me wisdom and life and breath,
> shepherd me far from the cliffs of death."

It may not sound like much, all that rhyming, but it was true and profound, large as eternity. I believe anything Jonas Caribou said in that voice of his would seem so. If he sang about the art of washing socks and underwear, it would be earthshaking.

When I left the room, that was it. Why should I share my stories, my penguin soul, with my children? Their souls are probably dried out and crumbling, pale and weak from neglect. If I could see them, I know that's what I'd find. No wonder they laugh.

I wandered upstairs. I've made a study in one of the rooms, bookshelves out of warped pine and cinder blocks, pieces of white muslin tacked to the windows to soften the light that pours through. It's moldy and damp, and it always seems like it's just rained in there.

I like to sit in my old, cracked leather chair, drink herbal tea, and read or think. The penguin recedes, and it's as if we've never met. Instead, I'm playing Chinese checkers with Walt again, or tossing the softball to June and Martha, who have to learn how to catch for their P.E. class. It's early evening, and the fireflies are just beginning to flicker, and I can hear the sound of someone's dog barking, of other kids playing up the street. But my children stay with me, and I'm one of them again, and we're together, as natural as the air.

———

Jonas talked about how we were all lost, all the time, but we didn't realize it. "Look up," he said, and we did, but I saw only the vast, pink-champagne ceiling of the conference room. "Your souls are right there," he said, "but you can't see them. Not now. By the end of the weekend, maybe. If you're lucky."

I couldn't wait. I thought my soul would be young, a full head of hair, smooth skin, charm and wisdom. We might have long conversations, and finally I would feel contained, self-contained and whole. I'd tell my soul my stories, and it would listen, nod, say, "I know, I know." And it would turn out that my whole life I'd never been alone, my soul following me everywhere, peering over my shoulder, laughing at my clever jokes and shaking its head in sympathy at my distant children and hard luck.

"Grab a partner," Jonas Caribou was saying, "someone you sense will understand you."

I looked around the room at the hundreds of people. They were turning to each other and talking, and the din filled the room. Someone tapped me on the arm. It was Myra of the evil shoulder blade. Not the person I thought would understand me best. But people were already joining up, and what if I told her no and ended up by myself?

Jonas led us through the exercise. We stood and held hands and focused on tunneling to the other's heart. It was hard work. Myra had gum disease, I'm pretty sure, and the odor made me lose my concentration. I kept seeing pictures of hospital beds and dentists, rows of teeth stored in jars.

I shifted my weight to my other leg.

"Ouch," Myra said. "Watch it. My shoulder—you have to be careful."

"Sorry," I said, and turned my head to the side to avoid her awful breath.

I bit my tongue concentrating so hard, and finally a real image came to me: a penguin, short legged, fat, waddling on some rocks, the sun glistening on his downy feathers.

"Myra," I said, "I see your soul. You're a—a penguin."

"No," she said, and it was the only time I saw her smile. "That's you. You're the penguin."

"What?"

"That's you—the penguin. I'm the teeth in the jar."

I stepped back. She'd seen the same things. Even though I hated to agree with her, it was amazing. It had worked, and this was only the first day. But then I thought about it—my true self was a penguin. An animal. Penguins don't even speak English. It would never understand me. I looked at Myra and she sighed, her breath making me reel.

"Every time I come to these things, it's the same," she said. "Same old jar of teeth."

I smiled weakly and turned to sit in my chair. That penguin was still walking around up there, in the air above my head, glorious in the sun, but somehow, well, undignified and a little short.

Once when I was holding Lila, she reached out her hands and placed them on each side of my face. June had run to the grocery store for more diapers, and Lila and I had been sitting for some time. She rested her hands on both my cheeks and looked at me, and I could feel her really looking, thinking hard. She saw me, I felt it, pure and uncorrupted, not me the father or the grandfather, nothing like that. My true self, without, I'm pretty sure, that penguin. She saw me the way my children used to.

Then Lila smiled and pinched my cheeks, and her new tooth showed. She drooled a little, but I didn't mind. Soon June came back from the store and took Lila from me.

"Stinky baby," she said, and set Lila on the kitchen counter while she unpacked her bag of groceries. "We've got to get you out of those clothes."

And Lila just looked at me and smiled some more, her face open, the front of her T-shirt wet with drool.

I wheeled the chair around and propped my feet on the edge of the shelf, in front of paperbacks by Adler and Jung, my ex-wife's old books, lent to me when we were still in college. Some day I really should return them. I leaned my head back and closed my eyes. The house was quiet, but I knew my children were still down in the living room, one of them suggesting they draw straws to see who would have to come after me. That's how it is now: I'm the booby prize. I hoped Stew would be exempt, since he isn't really family. I wished they would send Lila, but she can't walk yet. And anyway, she was with Stew's mother for the afternoon, decked out in fancy clothes and dress-up shoes, the way her grandmother loves her best.

I knew my children were whispering, "Damn it, Walt, you haven't had to go after him in years," or, "Martha, it's your turn." Even in their arguing they drew close, united against me.

I practiced my slow breathing exercises, the ones Jonas Caribou showed us. They're supposed to bring us to a meditative state, nearer our true selves. Inhale, one two three, release. And again. One two three, release. And then I knew, finally, in the middle of all that breathing, where it would end. Me hovering over them, watchful, waiting for the chance to be seen, and Walt, June, and Martha going on with their lives, never looking up to wave.

Farmer Boy

Let's say there was a boy named Farmer and he said E-I-E-I-O to the sky and his cereal bowl and his mother and the cars in the city. Talk normal, his mother said, but Farmer wouldn't listen. He never listened. He plugged his ears with his fat fingers and flicked his dull eyes. He did not know he would one day encounter disaster.

That day comes in winter. Farmer stands in the shower playing a game. He interviews himself.

Farmer, what would you like to be?

E-I-E-I-O

And how do you feel today?

E-I-E-I-O

Like your mother's cooking?

E-I-E-I-O

Like your father's square head?

E-I-E-I-O

Any question he asks, the answer is the same, different only in the inflection, in the emphasis. He sounds like a bad song, change that channel, turn that dial. But then, as he turns off the faucet, he yells something new. Ouch, he says, I've been bit.

True. One finger gone, eaten, no beast to be found. No bugs, no reptiles, no unkempt murderers with hacksaws behind their backs. Farmer's finger was gone. The space where it was, jagged and bloody, the only evidence and the only explanation.

Farmer moves toward the ridiculous, and I am supposed to have fun. Relax, my lover says, and stretches his arms over his head. He yawns and lies down on the couch, his legs so short he can fit without scrunching up.

"But Louis," I say, "I can't."

"Then don't," he says, "but leave me alone."

And so I do. Farmer rests in the corner, waiting for me to make up more. He doesn't care that it never happened, his story. I tell lies and time passes: one Mississippi, two Mississippi, three. I never knew Farmer and Farmer never met me. He would be easy to draw—his red nose and curly black hair, a mischievous stance, hands on hips, such sturdy arms. A well-fed boy. He wears suspenders and thick socks. He is out of style, from the past, but no one minds. People might sing to him: Farmer, Farmer, grow your crops, you're the Farmer, you're the tops. But they wouldn't mean it—he's just a boy. He doesn't know how to plant anything.

My mother calls while I am in the bath. I love to sit in the tub. These days, it's how I pass the time. I slide down low so my legs are bent, my chin touching the water, and I peer along the surface. I watch the water, its gray-blue cast, the ripples I form by moving my hand back and forth like a fin. Every sound echoes. The air is steamy, and breathing is suddenly important.

I fill the tub to just inches from the top. I don't plan on going any-where, don't think about much. I am that near weightlessness. It is as if I have never been born. So when my mother calls, I let her know it.

"I'm in the bath," I tell her. "I just got in. I'm dripping all over the kitchen floor. There's a huge puddle."

My mother sighs her huge, long, don't-worry-about-me sigh. "But you're always in the bath." I can hear her drinking something, prob-ably ice water. "Every time I call, you seem to be in the shower."

"No," I say, "I don't take showers."

"Whatever."

"So what did you want?" I am beginning to shiver.

"Oh, nothing. To see how you are. To see if you got my card in the mail."

My mother is terrified her letters will be intercepted. She en-closes a self-addressed stamped envelope with each one so she can hear back. I'm supposed to check the box next to Yes, I received your letter—thank you. But I never do.

"Yes, I did. Thanks," I say now.

"Have you been looking for work?"

"Louis works."

"But what about you? You need to work."

"Louis works," I say again.

"And you take baths."

"Yes. And this one is getting very cold." I hike my towel up under my arms, excuse myself. "All that water going to waste."

When I get back to the bathroom, the mirrors are covered with steam, but the water verges on lukewarm. I run more hot water, then pull the plug to let the level down a few inches, then run in still more water. I know I will stay in until my fingers are wrinkled—little pink prunes. For hours, maybe.

———

Downstairs, outside my window, the neighbors fight. I check to see that my door is locked. A car door slams, and I flinch. The woman stands watching as the man backs his car out and pulls away, the wheels screeching and churning, furious.

No one fights with me; I see to that. The thickness of my brick apartment walls, my calm lover. My Louis, always saying things like "We'll see," and "It depends." We talk in low voices, we compromise, we nod slowly and move carefully.

———

Farmer was embarrassed to show anyone his hand, the missing finger, the space where a fleshy index used to be. He even had to switch writing hands, but he learned quickly, and soon all was well. And then he could say two things: E-I-E-I-O and Ouch, I've been bit. He had dull eyes but he wasn't always stupid, not always—that's not what I meant. He learned quickly.

———

I dream that my mother bakes pie after pie, piling one on top of another: cherry, apple, pumpkin, pecan, lemon meringue. They sit on the counter, the buffet, the television, the end table by my couch.

Try some, she says, and smiles widely. Try some now. She slices into a blueberry pie and the blackbirds come flying out, just like in that kids' rhyme. In my dream, I am apprehensive about something, but I can't tell what. My hands shake; I'm not hungry. No, I say, I can't. My mother doesn't hear, though, and hands me a plate oozing blueberries. The pies surround me like a wall. I grow more and more nervous.

At first, after I wake up, I can't tell I've been dreaming. I think I smell the blueberries, hot and a little spicy, and then I realize I'm in my bed, the covers all in a wad at the bottom, Louis snoring softly beside me.

————————

So the mystery of Farmer's finger stretches out, a ribbon of road. Anyone's guess. What bit him? How did it get away? Did he do it himself? His mother tied a scrap of white cloth around the tip of his wound, and nightly he changed the dressing.

Do you think it will grow back? Farmer's mother asked the doctor.

If he is lucky, the doctor said.

And so the finger became as important as a jewel or a piece of art. It was only a finger, of course, but it was endangered. Farmer, his mother called, get off that jungle gym. Get off that slide. Get out of that tree. Come sit down. Relax.

But alas, Farmer was just a boy, only eight or nine, impatient. What did he care about his finger? It had stopped hurting, and so by now it must have healed. Of course it would heal, he was sure. Everything else—the skinned knees, the splinters, the stubbed toes—had always gotten better.

————————

The wild world outside, the possibilities. What could go wrong. A tree could fall on my car while it's stopped at the light. The elevator cables could break. I could get salmonella poisoning by leaning too long on the lunch counter at the diner down the street. Anything could happen. Lightning, small earthquakes, a spider bite. Someone could hold up the Rite-Aid. There's no guarantee for safety.

I know all this. My missing pocketbook, that dark night. A knife to my throat; I felt it shaking in the boy's hand. Take it, I said, there's lots. I held my pocketbook out, my arm straight. Here, I said, and dropped it on the pavement. And they did, just kids, they took it. They ran off into the dark, and one let out a whoop as they rounded the corner. I stood, petrified, trying to remember the way to my car.

At home I shivered under the covers all night, convinced they would come and find me.

———————

I grow old, I grow old, I shall wear the bottoms of my trousers rolled. Who said that? Was it Auden, Eliot? I have never had a memory for quotations, jokes, things people say, but this one rifles through my brain daily. I am only thirty, but why should I tell? Even Louis doesn't know; he's never asked.

I'm not old at all: see how my limbs still stretch, flexible, well muscled, see how my face is taut, clear, see my strong bones. But still, those words, they could be my mother's. You'll grow old. By thirty you could have five children. By thirty you could have a house and car. You could own stock in a major corporation. But I have plants, no children; an apartment, no house. Louis works at a jewelry factory, brings the supplies for the rings and necklaces and bracelets to the tables where women assemble them. He is the gofer; the women are not allowed to get up. He is a good lover, no boy, no friend, strictly the one I share my body with nightly. We have no plans, no map for the years to come. We steer steadily through the days, careful but unsure of our direction.

———————

The neighbors won't let their children play with Farmer anymore. Our father says you're strange, one girl says. Her sister stands by her side, chewing her braid. He says you're crazy. Get away from me, the boy from up the street yells, aiming his softball, ready to pelt him. But Farmer only growls. The children scatter, pumping their arms, running. They leave Farmer alone in his yard, where he is just as happy.

———————

Louis wants to get ice cream. He says, "Let's walk to the corner store and get cones. We can walk around the neighborhood." He paces the living room, his hands jammed in his pockets. "It's so stuffy in here," he says, "like the air needs changing."

But I like the walls around me, and I want to take a bath. I've been waiting all day. It's not right to take more than one, a waste of water, waste of time. "I like it here," I say.

"Come on." Louis stands in front of me, starts to pull away the book I'm reading, but I hold tight.

"Quit it."

"What is it you're reading, anyway?"

"A mystery." It's a thick book, hundreds of pages, and I am getting near the end. I'm about to find out who killed the twelve house-wives—a young, amoral boy or a crazed old man, the ex-owner of a traveling carnival.

Louis sighs. "Erina," he says, "it's been weeks since you left this place. You've got to come out sometime."

"I don't want to."

"What about work? How are you going to eat or get groceries? How are you going to pay the air-conditioning bills?"

I turn a page in my book, pretending hard to read, to look absorbed. "I've got some money saved."

"You've got some money saved." Louis shakes his head. "Great, great. And I'm supposed to pick up toothpaste or Q-tips, a bag of chips, something you're out of but can't bear to get for yourself."

"If you want."

"Well," he mutters, "we'll see about that."

I turn another page, nod. Louis storms about the apartment, putting on his shoes, stuffing his wallet into his back pocket. He grabs his keys and pauses at the door. "I'm going out," he says, and slams the door. The walls shudder. I hear his car start, and when it pulls out of the parking lot, the sound of the engine fading, I go to run the bathwater. I sit on the edge of the tub and watch the water rise.

––––––––––

Farmer hasn't been behaving. He threw a can of tuna at his mother. She slapped him and sent him to his room. There he brooded. He took his toys off the shelves and placed them in a pile, all the different cards and dice and plastic pieces mixed together. He sat in the middle of the pile, crushing little toy cars and paper-doll soldiers. He smiled at the mess he'd made. It's fun to be bad.

––––––––––

A year now that Louis and I have been together, and nothing changes. We begin and continue, the same the whole way through.

Louis would disagree. You seem more nervous, he says, and you never want to do anything. He says I'm afraid to go outside. He says this has got to change. But I like it here; I have all I need inside. Except for him. He comes and goes, and one day he might just be gone, never coming back. Gone in the morning and gone at night.

We could ride a carousel. If I'd leave the apartment. There's one in the park across town. I used to drive by it on my way to work at the Rite-Aid. I haven't been on one of those things in years, the horses slowly rising up and down, the metallic, greasy poles that hundreds of hands have clutched, and the corny music, the circus tunes.

If I could go there, the rest wouldn't matter so much—the wild world outside forgotten, all a blur passing by, the future no matter, the past no matter. I would only ride a few times. I would choose a horse with a curly mane and legs frozen in a gallop. And Farmer could come too, riding low in the back of my mind, holding tight, resting until I decided what to do with him next.

———————

Look, there it is, Farmer's been given the gift of speech. He acts more like a four-legged animal now, but see how his repertoire of words has grown. No longer just two phrases—several: None of your business, Shut up, Choke on your own phlegm, I'm hungry, and a few unmentionable obscenities entirely unsuited to a boy his age. His mother doesn't know whether to tear her hair out or rejoice. Sure, she's glad he can speak—she's always wanted him to speak— but these aren't the words she'd dreamed of. She can hardly write to the relatives and list his accomplishments. These aunts and uncles and two sisters live in the country, wholesome meals and clear complexions, and most importantly, children with impeccable manners. Farmer's father doesn't say much at all; in this way he's like his son. He's a stoic, a man's man, and who can say what he thinks at all? His son—a monster, a brat, it is all the same. He has work to do; let the mother be the mother.

———————

The man in the apartment next door plays the same song over and over, a woman's high voice singing, "You needed me, you needed me." He plays it every day in the afternoon, picks up the record needle and places it at the beginning again. I can hear the words through my thin walls. You needed me, you needed me. I think of Louis working hard at the jewelry factory, running to the McDonald's up the street to scarf down a burger on his twenty-minute lunch break. The woman on the record sings those words so many times that I begin to dream them at night. I consider banging on the wall or asking my neighbor to play something else, but he's clearly obsessive, playing that song—foolish? meaningful?—all day long. He can't be reasoned with.

———————

Ever since he had that disaster in the shower, Farmer gets naughtier still. He's become a rebellious child, problematic. He tosses his supper to the floor and stares at his mother, waiting for her fury to hit. He crawls around the house on his hands and knees at night when he's supposed to be in bed, crouches under the desk in his father's study. He claws at the furniture with his fat fingers, a harmless gesture, really, but difficult to watch. His eyebrows have grown thicker, closer together—odd looking on his little boy's face—and his fingernails need cutting. Cut them and you die, he tells his mother, spitting the words out. I'm growing them, he says. And what can she do? Every night, the food lands on the floor; every night, she bends tiredly, dishrag or paper towel in hand, to clean up the mess. She bakes Farmer chocolate-chip cookies and finds them stashed in the bottom of the tumbler by the bathroom sink, in the soap dish, or under a pile of towels on the clothes hamper.

Who are you leaving these for? she asks him one brave evening.

But Farmer just shrugs impatiently. He says snidely, An important visitor.

Farmer's mother places her hands on her thick hips, stands tall and luminous. Oh you devil-child, she says, and turns on her heels, leaving Farmer behind the shower curtain, mysterious in his bath.

———————

My mother calls again, the second time in a week, and I am sorting the clothes. Louis has promised to do the laundry, just this last time, he says.

"Do you have a job yet?" she says, her voice smooth but high, trying to disguise her concern.

"Not yet," I say, sorting underwear and socks into light and medium-light piles.

"Have you been looking?"

"No."

"What do you mean, 'No'?"

I imagine my mother pacing in her kitchen, alternately stirring something in a pot and sorting coupons on the table. This is how I almost always think of her: pacing, irritated, displeased about the smallest things.

"I've been busy," I say.

"With what? What could you possibly be busy with, alone in that apartment all day?"

"I'm making something." I think of Farmer, so bad, so clever, doing what he wants.

"Are you and Louis getting married? Because he could support you, I guess, since it looks like you're never going to work again."

"We're not."

"You're sure?"

"Yes." I sigh. "Look. I've got to go. I'm sorting the laundry."

My mother is silent.

"We're doing the laundry tonight," I lie. I know my mother will not approve of Louis doing it alone.

"Honey," my mother says, her voice soft, "it's only three-thirty. You have all the time you need."

"Still," I say, because I also want to take a bath, "there's really a lot of clothes. We haven't washed in weeks."

"You don't want to talk to me, do you? You don't like it."

"I do."

"What's wrong?"

"Nothing." I start on the towels, rough edged and smelling of mildew. The bedroom seems smaller, islands of clothes breaking up the floor into patches, some water here, a little there. I slump down on the bed, into the stale clothes I haven't sorted yet.

"Truly?"

"Yes."

After I hang up I don't feel like taking a bath anymore. I feel guilty, odd, watching myself and suddenly seeing how excessive, how unnecessary, a bath is. I burrow under the sheets, pull them over my head. My breathing seems loud, exaggerated in such a small, contained space.

Now Farmer says nothing at all—not E-I-E-I-O, not Ouch, I've been bit. He makes little grunting noises and crouches on the floor. He refuses to sit properly in a chair, and at the supper table he demands his food in a dish under his father's seat. Farmer's mother and father exchange worried glances, but they too say very little—as if by not speaking, they help hide the fact that their Farmer does not talk. At night they lie curled around each other, the father resting his head on the mother's chest. They whisper, What are we going to do? What have we done wrong? But in the morning, he is the same.

And Farmer's finger has not grown back. What is important is that Farmer leaves offerings of food—the cookies before, and now crusts of bread, half-eaten apples, a package of chewing gum, some oval pebbles—in the bathroom where he lost his finger. His mother finds them and throws them away, even the chewing gum, which she knows is not meant for her but for the thing that stole Farmer's finger. She hides her growing horror, tries not to imagine what goes on in her son's mind. She takes the cookies, the pebbles, the browning apples, and buries them behind the house. She buries them under a young tree. Maybe the tree dies, maybe it thrives. It remains to be seen.

Louis comes home late. I have fallen asleep on the couch, reading an Australian thriller I got for free when I still worked at the drugstore. I hear his key turn in the lock. He is startled, I can tell, that I'm not in bed, all the lights out, possibly snoring. His thin eyebrows jump high up on his forehead. "Oh," he says, "I thought you'd have gone to bed long ago."

"No. I was reading."

He sees the bags of clothes, stuffed full and leaning against the coffee table, the easy chair. "Hell," he says, and slaps his palm against his forehead. "The laundry. I forgot. I can't believe I forgot."

When he sits down next to me, I can smell his skin—new, someone else's smell, cigarettes and rose water and fried food.

"Where have you been?" I say. "Where'd you go all this time?" I stretch my arms, try to look nonchalant.

"I was out with friends." He looks at the world map on the wall. "You don't know them."

"I don't?"

"No. Friends from work. We ate out, saw a band at Lupo's, you know, that club we used to go to."

But I am angry. I don't want to hear about Lupo's, where we used to go, how much better it was then. The old days, when I would leave. The old days, when I couldn't see the need to beware.

"Well, what about the laundry?" I say. I put my feet on Louis's lap.

"I'll do it tomorrow. Or maybe I won't." Louis shrugs. "What if I don't do it at all? What if I say you have to do it?" He points his finger at me.

"You wouldn't do that, not after everything that's happened," I say.

"Might, just might." He nods. "Yes, I could see it."

––––––––––

Farmer lies on the ground and looks up at the sky. The clouds arrange themselves in the shapes of imaginary animals—griffins, sea serpents, two-headed toads. He grunts softly as they pass by in the strong wind. He's counting them as they change, as they shift into other, less interesting shapes, trees and houses and stop signs, or just plain amorphous blobs. He waves at each animal. He bids them farewell with his damaged hand, and all around him the green grass grows, fierce in the early summer sun.

––––––––––

Louis has left. I can't do anything for you, he said. I can't live two lives when I'm only one person. He hunched his shoulders and picked at a mole on the back of his hand. His one duffel bag, stuffed full, lay at his feet. As he left, he held the door wide open. Come out, he said. Erina, come out and stand on the stairwell.

But I couldn't. I shook my head, and then he turned and gently closed the door.

I walk around the apartment. I look out the giant sliding glass doors at the parking lot below. Sometimes twelve cars are there, sometimes three. The neighbors come and go, driving out into the city, the country, unseen places. I am here, keeping count, watching the only thing that changes in the view: the cars, how many, in which spaces they are parked, the yellow Volkswagen, the neutral gray and blue American cars, the van, the pickup truck.

Next door, the song still plays. You needed me, you needed me. What of it? I think. So what? The song plays and I tell myself it's just a song. It doesn't really matter. I settle into myself, into the fact that there is only me.

Farmer's mother found Farmer under the bed this morning. She came into his room around ten to open the shades and get him up; it may be summer but she won't have her son sleeping the day away. When she opened the door, she couldn't see him at first, but then she noticed his pudgy feet poking out from under the bed frame.

Get out from under there, she said. Come eat your breakfast.

Farmer scooted out and sat up, his hair covered with cobwebs, dust stuck to his pajamas. He rubbed a cobweb out of his one newly grown eyebrow and sifted his fingers together until the cobweb floated free, landing on the carpet.

I just vacuumed that, his mother said. I wish you wouldn't make such a mess lately.

And Farmer grinned and showed his yellowed, pointy teeth. Then you shouldn't have had me, he grunted, the first words he'd spoken in weeks.

His mother gasped and scowled.

Farmer got up, walked past his mother, past the orange flowered rug and the lamp shaped like a carousel, past the model firetruck he had built with his father, and down the hall. Shouldn't have had me, shouldn't have had me, he sang as he wandered all over the house.

What good is it, I ask you, what good is it? At night now, this apartment is silent. The walls seem to lean inward, the floor grows closer to the ceiling. And Farmer's not even real. He's just something I made up, neurons firing in certain directions. It all comes down to neurons. They make me sleep, they make me awaken. It's neurons that fire to make me afraid. My fear can be traced to a perfectly scientific explanation, a specific combination of fizzling and stillness all day long. My fear follows me, perched, I think, in the part of my brain that says Live, explore, be in the world.

There are options for the future, for what happens to Farmer. Either he becomes a fearsome, many-toed, single-eyebrowed animal, growling and cursing, or he dies a mutant death, curled up on his bed, the covers tangled at his feet. If he becomes an animal, he wins—not an actual prize, but some kind of invisible war. If he dies, it is his punishment, maybe for carrying on so, E-I-E-I-O, for being difficult.

I have given myself these gifts: Farmer, the mysterious creature of the bathroom, the doleful mother, the stoic father, what happens, what remains untold.

I sit and my coffee grows cold. I sit and the sofa creaks. My neck probably shrinks and then thickens; I stare out at the world like a turtle. Outside, the policeman three doors down is having a cookout. If I opened the windows, I could smell the smoked meat, barbecue sauce slathered over chicken. If I opened the windows, I could hear what his guests say. They nod to each other politely, offer each other beers from the cooler. One tilts her head toward the sky, her mouth open, white straight teeth, clearly laughing. They exude goodwill, good intention.

The policeman stands majestically at the grill, squirting more lighter fluid onto the coals, poking red embers with a stick. There is a slight breeze, and one woman goes to hold down a pile of paper napkins with a can of beer. I smile to see the world grilling chicken and laughing at the sky, eating potato salad off tailgates and nodding, satisfied, unaware that I watch from behind the curtain.

And then I do it. I slide the glass door open a little, just enough so

I can stick my head into the sunny outside, and I can feel the whoosh of fresh air on my face. I stand there, half in and half out of the room, peering down at the barbecue in the parking lot below. I am happy, relieved even, to smell the air, startling after the staleness of my apartment. I breathe for the first time in months, and right then it is all that matters.

Well, you can't see it, but Farmer's wearing a pot on his head, the popcorn pot, in fact. He's wearing the handle in back and jigging in the front yard. The neighbors peer through their calico curtains, alarmed at the quality of life on their street. They can't even remember what that boy was like before. They can't recall his bicycle-riding days or the color of his winter coat. They can't even remember his name. To them, he is the living example of the end of their good neighborhood—a kind of hex-burglar, cursing them with his wild eyes, his sudden movements, stealing their good image, their puffed-up pride in their streetlamps and evenly mowed lawns.

The pot nearly covers Farmer's face, and he is always pulling on the handle at the back to get a momentary view of possible obstacles—the mesquite tree, the pampas grass, the pecan tree, his father's sprinkler system. He smiles widely, and his feet hit the ground in an arrhythmic pattern, like a baby just learning to walk. He follows an unseen path, zigzagging and stumbling across the yard and back.

A disgrace; the neighbors begin to plot a way to rid themselves of Farmer forever. He must be weeded out like any other unwanted vegetable. Rotten heart, bad apple, this is the way they think. Anything's legal these days, let's trap him in a bomb shelter—he isn't human anyway. We'll bury him in the cornfield. Just get him out of our sight, most say. Fierce neighbors, each and every one, neighbors living beyond the normal scope of malice.

But Farmer doesn't care. He dances out there in the front yard, pot on his head, up in the morning as the sun is just peeking over the back of the house, there all day, wobbling and zigzagging, oblivious to the street, the other houses, the sky, the changing sun. No one will catch him. He dances, and the pot slides, and he fixes it, and he dances some more.

Star Seed

When one is a seed there is no worrying about the usual things. One does not have to prepare the meals, keep up with international affairs. One needn't try to remember the color of the past or decide whether or not to wear a raincoat. It's all the same inside an embryo, no fancy covering, nothing to write home about, but enough to do the job, good enough so that one can lie back and relax, stretch the arms over the head and yawn contentedly.

Julie's mother thought she was a star seed. She would knead her hands and stare past whoever she was talking to. "I am a special one, born into the wrong family," she would say. Julie didn't understand this, could not decide whether her mother meant the family she took care of now or the one in which she had been a child. Julie usually chose not to respond.

"Don't act like I'm some kind of freak who sees things in the air. I mean it, Julie. You're sitting there all quiet, but I'm telling you the truth."

Most of the time she hadn't said anything to make her mother think she didn't believe her. After a while, this was the way Julie came to listen to her mother: She asked many questions, nodded her head as if she were turning the answers over in her mind, asked where she could read up on her mother's real family, made no demands for scientific evidence. She could see the light shining in her mother's watery, introspective eyes, eyes that faced the wrong direction, inward, instead of toward the world.

A star seed should be taken seriously. No one can plant it, and it is not shaped like a star. It is shaped like Julie's mother, and it comes from a real star out in the universe. Sometimes it gets lost, as in her case, and must find the path back to its pod. "I'm lost," she said. "Get me a glass of water. I need to rehydrate." And so Julie was always bringing her mugs of water, goblets, brandy snifters, tumblers, anything, anything. Her mother must not go dry.

On the first day of winter vacation, Julie woke suddenly, startled. She felt someone staring. She looked up and there was her mother.

"I need to tell you good-bye. I'm going to New Mexico to find my pod family. I've read about New Mexico, and it's supposed to have more extraneous spirits than any other state."

The morning sun picked up red highlights in her mother's hair, and for a moment she resembled a movie star or a beauty queen, halo of brightness around her head. But her eyes squinted against the light, and her face was vague, as if she did not really know what she would do in New Mexico, or what to say next.

Julie propped herself up on her elbow. "What? New Mexico?" She rubbed half-dried sleep out of her eyes, wiped her fingers on the covers. "When did this come about, in the night?"

"I've been thinking about it. I've put in careful thought and hours of planning. This is not impulse, this is not irrational. I'm leaving tomorrow."

Julie said nothing, turned over, pulled the blankets over her head. She could feel her mother in the room, her slow breathing, the air faint with the scent of her cornhusk hand lotion. She grew damp and sweaty under the blanket, the roughness itching her face. She told herself, My mother wouldn't leave me behind, she couldn't. It's just a passing fancy, like when girls at school tie bright ribbons on their shoes instead of laces, a thing they feel sure of for only a few weeks.

But Julie was wrong. She could make such mistakes, had made them in the past, poor judgments of people, trust handed to bicycle thieves, secrets told to tattletales and gossips, friendships with idiot girls. She should have known it was real, that her mother was packing the car full of clothes, books on the nature of the star seed, a picture of Julie as a bald and drooling baby, candlesticks, a deck of cards. Whatever she could reach or see, could imagine herself using in some way. Frantic, grabbing, tossing things into boxes, jamming the flaps down, all in a hurry to get to New Mexico and meet herself.

Oren, Julie's boyfriend, thought he was quite something. He walked with a confidence rare in a seventh grader, a bit of a swagger combined with an aloofness that implied security. This was the natural state of his face: mouth almost bland, plain features changing only in moments of extreme anger or joy. But still, Julie knew he thought he looked okay; she had never seen him stutter or pull up his socks. If they hung around his ankles, that was that.

Recently, she had begun to feel silly thinking of Oren as someone she should love. She would never tell him her misgivings, but it was so. What was the point? She was only thirteen. Why bother? Clinging to someone whose initials were O.U.T.—Oren Upton Tipple—it seemed like bad luck, a way of hexing herself. But she did like him. He had given her a glass eye that looked more like a marble, with the swirls in the exact shape of an iris. The pupil was missing and the marble eye stared past anything, rolled off a table or across the floor.

"I bet this is a marble," Julie said. She watched the eye disappear under Oren's desk. They were in his room, not a speck of dust anywhere, the furniture arranged at right angles. His mother cleaned it every week.

He did not answer, his concentration focused on a song on the radio.

"And anyway, where would you find a glass eye? You'd have to steal it from someone, and that's no good. I've probably got inner-eyelid sweat on my hands."

"Baby baby c'mon kiss my toes. And if you like it I'll lick your nose," Oren sang, his voice off tune and scratchy.

Julie pretended she had not heard. "Some present. Either you lied and it's an old marble, or it's a glass ball covered with someone's eye snot."

He smiled, leaned over the side of the bed, scooped up the eye from under the desk. He blew on it and rubbed it against his shirt. "Yeah, well. I found it years ago in a package of marbles someone gave me. But it could be an eye. Anyone will tell you that's one thing they use marbles for. Those eyeless people need support. It's like bras or jockstraps, only everyone can see them. Glass eyes never look quite right."

So it didn't come from a half-blind man or a glass-eye factory. She was right, and she told him so. But Oren continued humming and Julie sat on the edge of his bed, and she did not care if his strict mother barged in and found her there instead of on the floor or in the orange guest chair. She hoped his mother would.

Julie's mother used to walk around the house singing rhymes she had made up about her state of being.

> Star seed star seed
> name I call myself
> Spent my whole lifetime
> sitting on a shelf

She sang to the tunes of old nursery rhymes, kindergarten songs—the wheels on the bus go round and round, I'm a little star seed short and stout, eensie weensie star seed crawled up the water spout, on and on, tunes that went in circles to end back where they had started. And so it was inevitable that she would drive away on a December morning, the car jerking into gear, the glare of the Texas sun, westward ho.

And all the time, meanwhile and meanwhile, Julie's father sat, one leg crossed over the other, his bearded bear's face, pipe in his mouth, reading philosophy and pondering. He stored his books on shelves with glass doors. They kept out the dust, he said, kept them in good shape, readable, ageless. He turned the pages carefully, holding the top right-hand corner of each page so he wouldn't rip it. When he dies, Julie thought, the books will be good as new. They'll be sold to libraries or bookstores for their full price. He was a philosopher king, he was a stoic, his pipe glowed orange in the early evening, he was thinking. And everyone knows that philosophers like to consider the possibilities of things such as seeds and pods, to lay out the premises and shift them here and there. But living with these seeds is another thing altogether.

In the classes he taught, students debated whether or not they existed, using as evidence the fact that they could feel pain, hear sounds, interact with each other, and die from gunshot wounds. Julie found these arguments pointless but gathered that somehow, in a way she did not understand, they were worrisome and mind boggling. She watched her father sit, one foot wriggling, the rest of him still, focused on the book.

"How can you just sit there?" She tried to keep her voice from rising to a high, childish pitch.

He looked up, blinked his eyes, surprised, she thought, to see her there. "What? What do you mean? I'm always sitting here."

"I mean," she said, and breathed slowly. "Aren't you going to talk to Mom before she leaves? Aren't you going to get the waffle iron back? She's taking the waffle iron, the one we use for our Sunday morning breakfasts." Suddenly this appliance, with all its lined-up squares, solid and heavy, seemed essential.

"We'll get another one."

"You're missing the point."

He tapped his finger against the cover of his book, restless, anxious to get back to it.

Julie moved her hands in small circles, rotating at the wrists, a bad habit. "She doesn't need it. She doesn't even know where she's going to live. She eats ground-up carrots and lettuce without dressing. Waffles are extravagant. They aren't even that good for you."

Her father grunted, nodded his head. Julie knew this meant he would consider it, which meant he would forget about it in a few minutes.

She began again. "Mom thinks she's a star seed."

Her father only nodded. "Yes," he said, "but there's nothing we can do about it. We can't change her mind."

Julie heard her mother rummaging through the cupboards above the kitchen sink, searching for vases and tarnished candleholders. She glared at her father, stuck her tongue out at his impassive reading head, and went to check on her.

She found her mother peering past the wooden salad bowls, the ones they never used, her feet planted in the sink so that from the doorway it looked as if her legs ended just below the calf. It was tiring to feel older than one's own mother, to be telling her to put the fake gold silverware back and to watch out that she didn't drop the cake-decorating kit on her head.

"You don't need that cake kit," Julie said. "Who do you know in New Mexico who has a birthday coming up? I bet you've never even met anyone from there."

"Well, you might come visit me. I might want to bake myself a cake. I might need it." Her mother turned, her hand on a pair of salad tongs. "How do you know what I'll need?"

"It's true, I don't. I don't know anything." Julie moved the magnetic letters around on the refrigerator door, pink and blue and plastic green. AHA! she spelled, two red A's and an orange H. And then, OH SHET. They had lost all the I's. SHET reminded her of Shetland, and she wondered who had named Shetland ponies. Where was the country of Shetland? She imagined hundreds of blond and stunted longhaired ponies grazing in unison.

"—so you might be able to reach one for me from where you are."

"What?"

"An apple. Could you get me an apple out of the fridge?"

"Sure." Julie reached in and found an apple next to a wilted head of lettuce. She tossed it upward. Her mother flinched, balancing in the sink and trying to catch the flying fruit. The apple landed on the floor with a soft thud.

"I didn't know you were going to throw it." Her mother's mouth turned down, disappointed.

"Sorry." Julie smiled, shrugged. She picked up the apple, held it over the wastebasket for a second, and dropped it in.

———

Julie loved to eat supper at Oren's house. The immaculate living room, the thick rug covering the floor, the knickknacks arranged perfectly on their stand—china dogs and crystal bowls, photographs of stately relatives. They added up to a place in which order ruled. She loved the way Mrs. Tipple rang a dinner bell, the "chime" she called it, when it was time to eat. She loved the fact that she and Oren had to wash their hands before coming to the table. Then Mrs. Tipple and Mr. Tipple and Oren would slide gracefully into their seats, place their cloth napkins in their laps, and Julie would sit down, too, following their example. When Oren picked up his fork, she picked up her own; when he reached for his glass of milk, she reached for hers. In this way they ate, the parents exchanging the events of the day, and Julie watching Oren to see what she should do next. This is what a real family looks like, she thought, this is what they do. They ring a chime and use cloth napkins, they use two forks instead of one.

———

Her mother was off, the blue Volkswagen bug sputtering. Julie stood next to her father. They both waved and waved. Anyone watching would have thought it was a celebration, the pecans strewn over the yard, the leaves piled along the curb, a kind of confetti.

Julie's father dusted off his hands. "Well," he said, and stared at the empty street. "New Mexico. I'm sure she'll like it." And then he turned to go inside, settle himself in the chair where he would read until early evening.

Julie picked up a handful of pecans, rolled them between her fingers. She chucked them into the street one by one. They bounced and rolled and came to rest against the neighbor's curb on the other side. Those neighbors hardly ever came home. When they did, they had an automatic garage-door opener so they didn't have to get out of the car. They just sat there, pressed the button, and the door went up, always at the same speed. She stood still for a moment, hands on her hips. Then she bent down, scooped up three pecans, squeezed them against each other until they cracked. She picked through the broken shells for the nuts. On the underside of one she found a worm, small and surprised, yellowish white. She dropped the nuts, wiped her hands on her pants. Her mother had really gone. She wanted to be sick.

———

At school she was not the smartest but she was not the dumbest either. She could answer a question if a teacher called on her, but she never raised her hand, eager to shout out that Sydney was in Australia, that you could find the circumference by multiplying two times pi times the radius. She had mastered an expression of perplexity, and when teachers looked around the room for someone to speak, they knew she was thinking hard. They usually asked Michael Harnigan instead; he looked them in the eye.

The first day after winter vacation, Mrs. Rockbow asked the seventh grade to talk about the things they had encountered during their break. "Encountered" was her favorite word. She also liked "challenge," "goal," "awakening," and the phrase "shine a flashlight on your soul." When she discussed the scientists who had discovered molecules and energy and DNA structures, she would say they were finding themselves in their work. She tried to make a connection between them and her students, who were finding themselves in their study of elements and compounds. Her lower lip twitched often and she checked her eye shadow in a compact at least once during each class.

"Bob?" she asked.

He smiled. "Mostly we raked leaves in the front yard. The wind kept blowing them around. And we bought ourselves a Ping-Pong table but now we don't know where to put it."

"Alicia?"

And so it went, around the room, up one row and down the next. Julie drew a pair of smiling lips and wrote the words "Heh heh, ho ho, hoo hoo hooooo" coming out the left side. She thought maybe it would be great to say she had taken a parasitic lover, and that every time she wanted to talk to him she had to get out a microscope. She felt pretty good for a moment.

Behind her, Alex told about his ski trip to Colorado. His mother and father had gone steady in this very junior high school, had met in eighth grade and were still together. His was the kind of family that took ski vacations every winter, wore matching ski suits and reflecting sunglasses.

Her turn now. She took the pen cap out of her mouth. "Nothing."

Mrs. Rockbow's lip twitched. "Nonsense."

"Okay, okay," she said, nodding. "My mother has been converted to a new species."

"And what species is that?"

"A plant."

And people laughed, it was a joke. Mrs. Rockbow was not amused, the routine of reporting encounters broken. Julie looked around the room, pleased with the result. Anyway it was true. Her mother had said so.

Leaning back in her bed, she often thought, I must tilt into another time, rest against something, how it used to be, my father getting out of his chair to buy groceries, visit the zoo, give lectures in other cities. My mother teaching first grade, cutting out pieces of felt to make bulletin-board exhibits. I know there was a time before this. But she also remembered all the silent suppers, her parents focused on their meals, saying nothing but "Pass the salt" and "Are we out of bread"; her mother sleeping until one on weekends; the house quiet except for the sound of each of them shifting and breathing. The silence enveloped them like snow.

She closed her eyes and opened them quickly, fluttering her lids, her own strobe light. She wondered if she could flutter them all the time. The sidewalk jerking slightly, the light strange and sharp, she'd have to take care to see where she was going, not to walk in front of cars, run into any old ladies. She'd have to move a lot slower.

They wrote several letters. Julie asked many questions, said little about herself: Mom. If you're a star seed how come you're always talking about the seed part but not the star part? Maybe you're just a seed. Grandma Piercy called—that's your mother, remember?—to see how you are. Julie.

Her mother wrote back that the air in New Mexico felt different, less moisture, more to breathe. She talked about a famous ranch where a woman named Georgia O'Keeffe used to live. When Julie looked her up in the library, she found pictures of whitewashed bones and strangely luminescent animal skulls. She was not impressed. What did it have to do with anything?

And Julie began to think this way: in vagueness. Someone, everyone, all the time, never. Rules she made up, laws of nature. Cats never fall out of trees. Girls can sense earthquakes better than boys can—in this she considered herself lucky. No one likes the color green even though it is everywhere. People who are in love are just in love and that is all. Who could say, who knew, it was all different, she had nothing to add.

Her mother hadn't always said she was born into the wrong family. She used to drink ginger ale and milk, wine coolers, hot chocolate—other beverages besides water. She seemed happy enough teaching hazy six-year-olds, having her one daughter, her pensive husband, her garden. But there had been clues. She was good at gardening and at knowing when it would rain. Proof, she would say now, that her seed instincts had already taken hold. Also, she had been the one to buy Julie a Junior Astronomer Star Man Telescope for her eleventh birthday. "You can learn all those constellations. It's good conversation for when you're older and out on a night walk with a boy and you can't think of anything to say," she had said.

The best thing about her, of course, was her temperament. Her face never grew red, contorted, furious. She demanded nothing tricky or hard to master. Julie's father said her patience could calm a volcano, which meant only that it was unusual. It stemmed, Julie knew, from her absentmindedness. She constantly forgot to put the gas cap back on the car, and she could not remember the way to the junior high school when it was her day to carpool. At the grocery store she bought five cans of tuna on sale when ten were stacked snugly in the pantry at home. Cause and effect bore little relationship to each other, floated out and alone. "Details, details," she muttered, and, "It all gets done anyway."

So she understood chaos, befriended it. She liked hailstorms and blackouts, shadows of the candles dancing eerily on the walls, the three of them eating popcorn on the couch and waiting for the power to return. Her mother liked all these things, didn't she? Well, didn't she? Julie could no longer say for sure. Maybe all along her mother had felt odd, left out, bored even. Maybe she was a secret and very good actress. The seed business served as a mask; she ran away to a drier climate. She went, Julie thought, with her arms slightly outstretched, palms up, panic on her face, small mechanical steps taken quickly.

New Mexico is a state made up of two words, and Julie did not wish to say more about it.

"But why New Mexico?" Oren asked.

"Because." She didn't know.

"Because why?"

"No one knows."

"Except your mom." Oren bit down on a cinnamon jawbreaker, pulled a leaf from a low-hanging branch. They were walking back from the 7-Eleven, where they had bought two dollars' worth of candy. His mouth made sucking noises, and Julie could hear the candy clicking against his teeth.

"No one knows, not even her. That's the way it is." She spread her hands, fingers splayed, for emphasis. "Hand me a Tootsie Roll, will you?"

"But she might know. I mean, have you asked her?" Oren reached into the brown paper bag, pulled out a butterscotch. "Here. I ate all the Tootsie Rolls." He put his arm around her, his cinnamon breath near her ear. He kissed her temple, loud, wet.

"Hey!" She jerked away, smiled. "Your lips are bright red."

At home her father had fallen asleep, his mouth sagging. A bit of saliva dappled the edge of his lips, and his book lay open in his lap.

"Hello, Mr. Dillon," Oren said.

He did not answer.

"My sleeping dad," Julie explained.

"Yeah."

Julie wanted Oren to leave. She wanted to lie down on her bed and watch the ceiling, the pockmarks and cracks arranging themselves into designs—amoebas, constellations. "So," she said, "I'll see you later. Get out of here and we'll talk tomorrow."

Oren nodded. "Right. Tomorrow." And he was out the door, leaving it open behind him. The mild February air shifted in the living room, lifting a few pages of a magazine on the coffee table. Then Julie shut the door and everything was still.

Her father began complimenting her on the wrong things. He had no sense of what came accidentally and what had been earned. For example, he said, "Your nose is very becoming," or, "It's good to see you're doing all your homework." But she always did her homework, the path of least resistance, no pink slips sent home by displeased teachers. And her nose was Grandma Dillon's; anyone could see this in the portrait in the hallway. A genetic thing, a fluke, the DNA twisting just so. Julie noticed these compliments at their awkward suppers together, the two place mats across from each other, the food arranged in the center of the table, so much space, so much time surrounding each sentence. Her father wielded his fork and knife carefully, avoiding the embarrassing possibility of food in his beard.

"Thanks," she said, knowing that soon he might compliment her on her fine manners, the fact that she chewed with her mouth closed, answered the telephone with a calm hello.

Then they moved on to other subjects.

"How's Oren?" he asked.

"Fine."

"That's good. He's a nice boy. You have good taste." He drained his glass of milk.

"Yeah, thanks. Yeah, he's okay." She picked at her sweet potato, slicing it into triangles and rhomboids. Oren was probably having some kind of gourmet chicken dish with a French name for supper.

"Got a letter from your mom today."

"Oh yeah?" Julie noticed that he did not call her mother "Anna," which he had always done before. Guarded, they were so guarded, she thought, neither of them wanting to slip, to seem too anxious.

"She wants me to take some pictures of you so she can put them on her wall."

"I don't want to," she said. "If she were here she wouldn't need pictures. She could see me every day."

Her father said nothing, reached for the salad.

Julie fidgeted, began to shred her napkin. "Did she find an apartment?"

"Yes," he said, clearly relieved. "And she gave us her address, so we don't have to send letters to that motel anymore."

Julie knew he detested the thought of her mother staying in a Cactus Inn. Seven weeks in a motel, he had said, and shook his head.

"And she's looking for teaching jobs at all the elementary schools." Her father paused. "You should be nicer to her, Julie."

"I am," she said. "I am nice." She pushed the pieces of potato to one side of her plate, pressed her fork into them, crisscrossing. So her mother really would stay, the permanence implied in the job.

Her mother, stolen away by a theory about pods, stupid things that grew out of the ground.

There are many places in the world, all existing at the same time. Even in one person the places are numerous. There is the place we go at night in our sleep, and the place we call our home, where we take showers and eat meals. What we imagine to be other places even if we have never been: China, a swimming pool in Germany, the inside of the house next door, the way the woods must look to a wandering dog, the pictures that flash into other people's heads. If we think of all these places, all at once, all those people eating breakfast—their cereal or their bacon or their millet or dirt, or other things we cannot imagine—if we think of them while we are only ourselves, we become paralyzed, turn to stone, our little brains confused to consider so much at once.

And so for Julie it felt good to look at the ceiling, white, marked with odd, inconsistent swirls of paint. She did not consider what her mother might be eating for supper, who she talked to, what her new apartment looked like. She reasoned that a month was a long enough time to hang the few pictures, line up the shoes in a neat row or throw them into the closet, hear them tumble against each other, find the mice lurking in the kitchen drawers—enough. She hoped her mother was sorry for leaving, missed everything about her past, felt as lost as a sea gull in Nebraska. She told herself, Everyone must go on at least one quest.

In fourth period one day, Julie got a note from Oren. Ellen Potentoch, who had math with him the period before, handed it to her. "He says to read it right away," she said, smiling. Ellen had bad breath, like old toothpaste, and she giggled too loudly.

"Thanks." Julie took the note, haphazardly folded to the size of a matchbox. Oren's handwriting, all capital letters and straight lines, read, Joo, Meet me at four and we can ride our bicycles through the graveyard. Love, yer O.

"The graveyard, huh? Pretty weird if you ask me." Ellen was leaning on the back of Julie's chair, reading over her shoulder.

Julie squinted her eyes into her most hateful look, shook her head slowly back and forth. "I didn't," she said in a low voice. "And if you tell anyone, your name is blood." As an afterthought she added, "And quit breathing on me."

That afternoon she found an unopened letter from her mother on the buffet. Her father was teaching class, lecturing on the nature of uncertainty and how it indicated good. Her full name scrawled—Ms. Julie Dillon. The "Ms." made her feel young, unreal, like a new shadow. The envelope was taped closed but she ripped the flap, destroying it. The letter only took up a few lines. It read, Dear Julie, I am sorry if you don't believe me when I say I know what I am doing. I have been your mother for thirteen years and you know I have never been that bad at it. I am teaching first grade and reading a lot of books. I have decided I have a problem with boundaries, but that is not so unusual. Please write and tell me what you are up to. Love Mom.

Julie imagined her mother bumping into walls and walking past No Trespassing signs, constantly saying, Sorry, Sorry, Oops. Her father, on the other hand, thought with grace and moved slow as an elephant. Her hesitant mother, her pensive father, their boundaries, their love getting bumped and crushed, stomped on the floor by accident. Sorry, they must have said, Oops, they must have muttered, bashful, relentless in their mistakes. Star seed or no star seed, her mother would never come back. Her father would continue to turn pages. They would all grow older.

Julie crumpled up the letter and stuffed it in her jeans pocket. She had to get out of there, the house still and guilty, the secrets of all that had transpired hidden within. She rushed down the front steps two at a time and jumped onto her bicycle. She pedaled down the driveway, gathering speed. Dogs barked frantically as she passed their yards. You blind, stupid girl, they seemed to say, she's never coming back. They barked and ran the lengths of their chain-link fences, and Julie turned down Oren's street, gripping the handlebars tight.

The graveyard was two miles from her house, filled with dead soldiers, all the headstones shaped the same, equally spaced in long, perfect rows. They reminded Julie of giant lost teeth, chalk white and blunt edged. Riding her bicycle with Oren, she did not grow tired. She felt she could speed along at a hundred miles an hour, journey for days. She could barely keep her feet on the pedals, they revolved so quickly. She was taut, strung like a tightrope, nothing to spare. A furious rider, the racing daughter of a star seed. A seed who didn't love her husband, who had a problem with boundaries, whatever that meant, who lived in New Mexico and raved about a place called Ghost Ranch. Julie barreled along the path, she rolled smoothly, the graves flying by, blurring into columns of white.

"Wait! Hey, slow down. Hey!" Oren called, his voice faint in the distance.

She had forgotten him. She slowed, felt the tiredness in her legs. She looked at the ground a few feet in front of her, saw the dried twigs and the brown bits of grass mowed weeks ago. The cemetery yardman would get into trouble, she thought, all those generals and colonels liking clean paths and no debris. Oren pulled up beside her.

"What're you doing riding like that?" he said, red and huffing, sweat trickling down his neck.

She looked at him.

"Really. I mean it. I thought we were riding together, you know, two people going on a ride. That doesn't mean one person takes off and rides like she's in a race. It means we ride along and talk and stuff." Oren's face was odd, all red like that, such a rare sight.

"Sorry," she said. "Sorry, I forgot. I just needed to, um," she pulled a piece of hair out of her face, "ride like that for a minute."

"A minute—you mean ten."

"Huh?"

"Ten minutes. Ten at least, you took off as soon as we left my house. I bet you didn't even stop for the stoplights."

Julie nodded. "Yeah, well, I'm fine now. I can see some stuff I didn't before." She braked, hopped off her bicycle, clanged the bell on the handlebar, walking.

Oren weaved and teetered, trying to ride as slowly as she walked. "Like what?"

"Things." Nothing to do with seeds, she thought, much to do with separation. She imagined her parents nodding at each other in the night. Oh well, they would have said, it didn't work out. Gosh, they must have apologized, I thought you were my one and only. No screaming, no fighting, no pushing, no biting. A quiet sneaking apart, and she had never seen it.

She turned to Oren. "I know I exist if my legs are tired from all this bicycling, right? Because I can feel it, right? It means I have sensory perceptors, and that they're working."

He shook his head. "What?"

"Right?"

"You've been talking to your dad too much. That's just mind stuff. It doesn't mean anything. Obviously you're here or you wouldn't be walking your bicycle next to me."

Of course he was right. But she hadn't been able to see any of that. She climbed onto her bicycle. She pictured the blood pumping through her veins, traveling to her feet and her brain, her gums and even her earlobes. She thought about the way her parents must have discovered they no longer liked living in the same house, calmly, as if they had read it in a book, not thinking of the actions that would follow the plan. Not bothering to tell her—afraid, maybe, yes, that she would not be so quiet, so compromising. The blood moving slowly through them, their heart rates solid, unexcitable.

"Well," she said, "let's go home." Her legs ached. She felt drained, all the fury sucked from her. They passed the graves, leaves crackling under their wheels, and pieces of gravel popping out from underneath. There would be things to say to her father tonight, words to drop into the smooth surface of their evening conversation. She would send out ripple upon ripple, her new life fraught with a sore heart, the rage at having been left so suddenly.

Camping with Strangers

In a dream last night I saw myself as a baby. I watched myself totter around the backyard in red overalls. I could barely walk, I was very young. The best thing about me was my eyes. They were blue like they've always been, but they shimmered, and I looked wise. My baby self stared at me, blinked her eyes significantly, turned to put a stick in her mouth. I thought, Oh how intelligent, that expression, but then I grew worried: the fine hair, the wavering, what was she trying to tell me? My mother appeared behind me. Her hands felt cool and dry in this dream; she tapped my clavicle and rested her hands on my shoulders. "Enough," she said, "you have seen enough." She never showed her face to me—I felt her there and knew who she was. Then my baby self disappeared and soon I had only the blankets wrapped around me and the memory of my wise small eyes.

My mother knew I had no intention of spending my future with Artis. He hated most things—music, art, youth, giddy laughter, bright colors. He used to say if he were king of the world, he would kill all the humans and let the animals roam free. He envisioned them grazing in endless fields, drinking from clear streams.

"But, Artis," I would remind him, "there's pavement everywhere. Those animals would have to live in twenty-story buildings. They'd have to learn to climb stairs."

He sighed exasperatedly, gave me a look of disgust. "Whose side are you on, anyway?" he said. This was his favorite question.

During the time I spent with Artis, I became a teacup. He poured words and ideas into me, his feelings and opinions, insights and confusions—whatever he thought of. I listened until his words began to overflow like another language; I focused on the furniture in the room, the posters, a clod of dirt lodged in the carpet. But then he began to catch my mind drifting away from him—once, when he was talking about our future.

"Well, we need to make plans," he said, "lots of plans, big plans, the future, what we want. I think if we get married we could stay here. You like your job and mine's okay for now. It seems like all my friends are married so I don't see why we can't do it, too." He paused for breath.

I counted the number of electrical outlets in his living room. Five, including the one behind the couch for the floor lamp.

He continued. "I've been reading all about marriage in old European societies and I think we should do it up really big, lots of wine and good food. Your mom can make the poppy-seed cake we always have over at her house. We can crush goblets with our feet like in that movie, uh, what was it called?"

I didn't answer.

"Tamar? Are you listening?"

"Hmm? Yeah." I nodded my head, scrambling for the name of the film. We had seen it several weeks ago. "I don't remember, but I know what you're talking about."

Artis sighed. He picked up a magazine, thumbed through it. The pages fanned, he flipped so fast. "I'm practically asking you to marry me and you're not even listening. This is the big moment of any man's life, and you're looking at the wall."

"Sorry," I said. I reached over and touched his forehead. "I'm really sorry, okay?"

"Yeah." He paused for a moment, his dark hair falling into his eyes. "But Jesus Christ, what were you doing, counting sockets or something?"

And so you see, this was the thing about Artis: Even though I listened until his words blurred together, even though he rarely asked me anything about myself—despite all this, he could still guess what I was doing. An uncanny skill. He always seemed so self-absorbed. It surprised me every time, was enough to make me wonder if he were psychic.

One Saturday Artis and my mother and I went to what we thought would be a furniture auction—although the location should have tipped us off. Artis saw the ad in the newspaper and asked me if I thought my mom wanted to go.

"Maybe," I said, through a mouthful of cereal, distracted. When Artis stayed the night, I always felt like a part of me was missing the next morning, as if, over the hours, my center drifted away.

"It's at the sporting goods store, the huge one with the giant turning football on the roof and the mall-size parking lot."

"Okay," I said. But it came out wrong, I could tell the minute I spoke.

Artis picked a piece of lint from his T-shirt. "Well, it's this afternoon, so if we want to go we should call your mom. You know how she likes to plan ahead."

"Yep."

"You don't sound very excited."

"It's fine," I said. I reached for the front page of the paper.

"Look, if you don't want to go, just say so." Artis drummed his fingers on the table, jiggled one leg, getting nervous.

I looked at him, put my hand on his leg to hold it still. "Artis," I said, keeping my voice calm, "I want to go, really. You know I would say if I didn't." This was a lie; usually I told myself it didn't matter much either way. Time passed one way or another.

"Okay. Well, good. I was just checking." He stood up to take my bowl to the kitchen. "Do you want to call your mom so we can go?"

"Yeah, in a minute."

"Soon."

"All right, all right," I muttered, and shook the crease out of the newspaper.

The auction was not selling the usual furniture—no antique lamps, heavy walnut buffets, corner cupboards with glass doors, nothing like that. The sellers had placed a tricky ad in the paper: "Furniture & Other Delectables." But what they meant, in fact, was lawn furniture, pop-up chairs a foot high, the kind older people take on picnics so their backs won't tire, swing sets, hammocks, sports equipment. We had driven to the corner of Maywell and Offer

Streets and found ourselves in front of the sporting goods store with a circus tent pitched in the middle of the parking lot.

"Oh, no," Artis said. "Commodification of the great outdoors."

"What?" I said. He always used terms like that even though I told him again and again no one got it. "Say what you mean."

My mother reached over the front seat for the paper. "We must be in the wrong place. Tamar, let me see that ad."

"No, this is it," I told her. "Look, there's the sign. Auction. We're here." Artis and my mother stared at me. "Well, we might as well take a look," I said. I opened the car door and started for the lot. They followed a few yards behind.

Inside the tent we found it. A man on stage spoke quickly, his words rushing into each other, blending together in monotone—Artis's speaking style magnified ten times. He held up a kerosene lantern, said five dollars, five five five, six dollars. I concentrated to recognize the point at which one word ended and the next began. While he waited for two men in gimme caps to bring up the next item, he flipped the cord of the microphone up and down like a whip. I watched, mesmerized, as he began the next sale. He pointed to a sleeping bag, deep green with three sets of zippers and double stitching.

"This Woolly Worm sleeper will keep you warm even in the Arctic," he said.

Then the bidding began. People held up cards with their numbers printed in thick black ink, took them down, held them up again as the price rose. The sleeping bag finally sold for 125 dollars, a bargain, the woman in front of me mumbled. The auctioneer banged a miniature gavel on his stand several times.

Artis tapped me on the shoulder. "Here, I got us numbers. We're registered. Now we can buy something if we want."

My mother laughed. "What would we want with all this outdoorsy stuff? I've never needed a sleeping bag in my life and I don't intend to get one now. All those years I worked so I could live in a house—I'm not giving that up, no way."

"Yeah, but it might be fun," Artis said. He handed me a card. "Here's your number, Tamar."

"Thanks." I looked at my number, 137, scrawled in black permanent marker. I breathed the fleeting, chemical odor of the ink.

On stage the two men set up a light blue tent, complete with a rain fly that had a nicely contrasting navy sheen. The metal poles bent slightly, molding the roof of the tent into an arch. It brought to mind the windows of medieval castles, the wooden doors of ancient Spanish missions in the Southwest. I imagined the tent on a field of grass, green and lush, all the same height, little drops of dew on each blade. I saw the sun rising soft and orange, the way it does in commercials for deodorant and vitamins. And I knew I had to have that tent. Oddly, I did not envision the inside of the tent, the blue cast the light would have, the condensation on the walls in the morning, the humid air. I thought only of the bold blue, the inviting orange, the silver of the dew, and the carpet of grass.

"One forty, one forty. Number eighty says he'll take it. Higher? We can go higher. Ninety-one bids one sixty. At one sixty now, one seventy-five. At two hundred now."

I raised my card in the air.

"One thirty-seven, lady in the back, wearing brown. One thirty-seven bids two hundred."

Artis looked at me, surprised. "You don't have that much money. You're always telling me how you're broke."

"It's a glorious tent." That was all I could think to say.

"We don't even have sleeping bags," he said.

"I've got plenty of blankets. Maybe we could safety pin them together."

"It better be some tent," my mother said. "I've already told you I'm not lending you any more money."

"Two hundred," the man called.

I raised my card again.

"Two hundred—no more takers? Two hundred going once." He paused. "Two hundred going twice." He banged his gavel. "Sold to number one thirty-seven."

I clapped my hands, ecstatic, as if I had won something on a game show, and wove my way through the crowd to the registration table to write my check and pick up the tent.

"It's a good deal, don't you think?" I asked Artis when I returned.

He fished the wadded-up piece of paper with his number from his jeans pocket and tossed it over his shoulder. "I guess."

"Hey, Mr. Environment, you're littering."

"It's only cement. The ground underneath this parking lot is dead anyway."

I shrugged. "Whatever. Look, if you want, you can come over sometime and we can set up my tent in the backyard."

"Yeah, maybe."

My mother berated me all the way home. "Even when you were a little girl," she said, "you were an impulse buyer. All those toys you only played with once and then left out in the rain to ruin. You never cared about them for very long." And more about how I needed to prioritize, recognize my responsibilities, buckle under and get serious.

"Okay, enough, enough," I told her, "I'm twenty-three, not five." And we rode the rest of the way home in silence. I held the tent in my lap, satisfied with its weight, wondering how it would look in my backyard.

I was a girl with little to say. My friends bossed me effortlessly. I played the family dog in games of House, the grandmother quickly eaten in Little Red Riding Hood. At school I gave away my lunch dessert to anyone who asked, even if my stomach had rumbled all through the morning. I couldn't have cared less about getting the answers right in class, and at home my mother constantly reminded me to pull up my socks, arrange my barrettes evenly in my stringy hair, stand straight, smile more often.

My father took a train to Canada eight months after my birth, never returned, sent no postcards or crisp twenty-dollar bills. My mother and I did not discuss him one way or the other. The one time I asked her about him, she said, "It doesn't matter. He doesn't love you and I do." It probably does matter, but she says there is nothing to tell, and so I am stuck with just the four facts: he was my father, he took a train to Canada, he never came back, he never made contact. Summed up quickly they appear innocuous.

"You should find a good man," my mother has always told me. And implicit in this is the story of my trickster father who disappeared in the night, her wish that I do better, but also her conviction that I am not capable of such things.

We made an unusual couple, Artis and I. He has dark sticky hair, very thin, which he can mold into any shape with his hands. And on his forehead there is a vein, running straight up the middle from the point where his nose begins, level with the eyebrows, to his hairline. Sometimes I traced it with my index finger, but after a while I had to stop. Artis said it made him nervous, told me it was bad luck—might cut off his circulation or hurt his thinking process. I used to tell him the vein was so prominent that his brain must be in his nose, but he didn't find this amusing.

I'm a sliver under six feet—a few more layers of skin on my heels and I'll be there. Artis, in moments of kindness and inspiration, told me I could be a model, but of course this is a thing one tells one's tall lover. My limbs stretch out, long and spindly.

But all the same, friends and relatives, acquaintances who saw Artis and me for no more than five minutes, clerks in department stores who rang up our purchases—all these people told us, "You two make the perfect couple." I saw it in their eyes even when they didn't say anything. It is the same expression people have when they see a scene that pleases them: good color composition, ample space between objects, no chaos, one thing blending into the next. Their eyes close slightly and they nod, and then they smile.

We did not match, it should be obvious, but no one could tell except me. For a long time I thought of the story about the emperor's new clothes and wondered what really happened to the kid who pointed a finger and called the king naked. Surely no one believed him, surely they cut off his head and hung it on a fence post as an example. Probably the parents tried to hush the child, but it was too late.

At night when I was falling asleep, Artis's arm under my neck or across my belly, all I could think of was the tent. It had been sitting on the floor by the front door for two whole weeks.

"Maybe we should set it up tonight," I told Artis one night. He was nibbling at my ear, his wet tongue on my lobe. I couldn't stop myself thinking of my ear, enveloped by a pink, slimy thing. Not that I didn't like it—I just kept seeing in my mind how we looked. I felt silly, old.

"Now?" Artis drew back, pushed some hair from my face. "You want to put it up now? We're in bed."

"Okay, okay," I said.

We lay there silent for a few minutes. The heater clicked on and off, and I began to grow sleepy. The covers wrapped tight, Artis breathing next to me, a little wind outside.

"Tamar?"

"Um hmm." I stretched my hands over my head and turned on my side away from him, taking some of the blankets with me.

"Nothing." Artis reached up, turned out the light. "I can see you're thinking."

In the morning I woke to find Artis at the kitchen table doing the daily crossword puzzle. He was hunched over the newspaper, an afghan draped over his shoulders. I put water on to boil for tea.

He looked up. "I need a definition for 'parameter.'" His hair stuck up in thin spikes.

"I don't know," I said. "There's a dictionary by my desk."

Artis shook his head. "Nah, I'll just do the next one. Seven down. Do you know anything about opera?"

"No." I handed him a banana. "Here. They're going to be too ripe tomorrow."

"Me neither." He folded the paper so that it looked as if no one had read it and slid it into the plastic bag it had come in.

We sat and drank tea, peeled the speckled skins away from our bananas, ate in silence. It was not the contented silence of people who know each other well, who can converse in sighs and periodic nods of the head. No, we missed each other night and day, spent our skewed lives tripping through our awkward kisses, our muddled conversations.

My favorite card game is solitaire. I love to line up the cards, the seven piles, each one larger than the last, the first card turned face up for promise, for potential. I play one game and if I lose I must play another and another. But first I shuffle the deck. I heard on the radio that the best way to shuffle a deck, to make sure all the aces are well distributed, the kings not stuck together, is to do it seven times. My cards have become tattered and bent, and one of the twos has a corner missing, so they are no good for playing poker or gin—someone could cheat, it wouldn't be fair. But they're my favorites. I got them on a plane. The stewardess plunked them down on my plastic table with a package of peanuts. Here you go, she said in a tired voice. I felt personally lucky—she only gave them to every other passenger. I guess we were expected to share with the person next to us, start up a game of Go Fish or Crazy Eights. The man next to me snored softly, his mouth open, his hat on his lap. I slipped the cards into my bag and he never knew what he was missing.

Thoughts run through my head while I play. I will be setting down a queen onto a king, will have just turned over another ace to put up top, and I will remember a dream I had or a bad thing I did when I was little, my first date in high school, what I will do next weekend. The last time I played, I remembered all the way back to when I was four or five years old, when these boys in my kindergarten class said we would play a game. It happened during recess. They told me they had little candies shaped like aspirins, those baby aspirins our mothers used to give us. The candies came rolled up in a piece of cellophane—Smarties, they were called—in pastel pinks and yellows and greens, some purples.

So they said we were playing Sick Person, and that they had come to save me, the sick one. First, they said, open your mouth. I did, and a boy in my car pool dropped a Smartie onto my tongue.

I feel better but I probably need another one, I told him. But then the biggest boy, Rodney Powell, who turned out to be a bully later on in middle school, said, No, first you have to take off your panties.

Thinking about it all these years later, playing solitaire, I realized they probably expected me to protest, and that would have been the end of that. But I said okay, and I unbuckled my jeans and pulled them down around my ankles. I don't know what I was thinking in my five-year-old brain, how I must have felt. It was February, I remember, and I could feel the cold wind on my legs.

Those boys, though, they all at once turned and ran. I stood there, pulled up my pants, buckled my belt, slightly confused, I guess. They hadn't even given me another piece of candy. Probably I felt gypped, ripped off, so much trouble for nothing. Probably I didn't understand that most nice kindergarten girls would have scrambled full speed out from behind that hawthorn bush, crying for the teacher. I didn't know that the thrill of the game, Sick Person, lay in the danger, in the proposal of shocking acts, of which none of us, I am sure, had any inkling.

So playing solitaire I am grateful. Aha, I think, here we have it, the first visible sign that I will grow up to be a flippant woman, nonchalant in my desires, fickle as dust, settling wherever I happen to land. I shuffle the cards, revel in the way they slap against each other and collapse in my hands.

My mother called me a few days after I bought the tent. She said she was just checking what time we'd be over for supper on Tuesday.

"They had a special on pot roast at the Bestway," she said. "We haven't had roast in forever."

"Okay," I said, although pot roast is not my favorite. "That sounds good."

Then the questions began.

"What were you thinking when you bought that thing?" she said.

I pretended not to know what she meant. "What thing?"

"The tent. Are you going to take Artis on a camping trip?"

"If I want. I just liked it, I don't know why. Do I have to have a reason?"

"You've never been camping in your life. You don't know the first thing about collecting berries or finding sticks for a campfire," she said.

"Kindling—it's kindling. Anything else?" I said. As we talked, I rolled a miniature car I had found on the sidewalk back and forth on the table. It had doors that opened and a purple coat of paint. I pushed it to the end of the table so it teetered on the edge, then back to the center, near the salt and pepper shakers.

"No. I'll see you at six. If you have time, could you pick up a bottle of dish detergent? I'm out."

"Sure."

"Well, actually, one other thing. I've been meaning to tell you, and I know you won't like it."

This is the way my mother always prefaces her most difficult advice. "Sure," I said, my voice impatient.

"You should be nicer to Artis."

"What?" I couldn't believe it.

"You don't treat him right."

I wanted to hang up. "Gotta go, Mom," I said, and I did.

I sat at the table. It's true, my mother's eye follows me everywhere. But she had never told me how to treat a boyfriend. I thought of her eye in my bedroom at night, disapproving, blinking while Artis and I removed our clothes and wrapped ourselves around each other, the darkness closing in around us, the only time we truly compromised.

On the day I had decided to set up my tent, I woke to the sound of rain beating against my bedroom window, uniform, relentless. I had invited Artis over to witness the great ceremony. If we like it, we can go camping when it gets warmer, I told him.

I set the tea kettle on to boil, ran down the front walk to grab the Sunday paper, soggy, tearing apart in my hands. Muddy water streamed down the street, the ground already saturated. There was no way I would pitch my tent in a yard of mud. My backyard has no grass, and the landlord said it was my fault. The pet ducks I once owned scourged every blade, every seed, leaving me only fine, loose dirt covered with dead leaves in the fall. One day the dirt will erode completely, leaving me with nothing but the underground plumbing and a few confused tree roots.

I dialed Artis's number, let it ring eight times, dialed again.

"Hello." His voice was slow, sleepy.

"Hey, it's me," I said. "Sorry I woke you up."

"It's all right." He yawned. "What's up?"

"Well, it's raining out, I don't know if you noticed, and today's the day we were going to pitch my tent, remember?" I talked through the silence on the other end. "My backyard's a lake. We'll ruin the tent."

"Okay," he said. "Okay. Some other time, then."

"Wait," I said. "I thought we could set it up in my living room. The frame will hold the tent together—of course, we couldn't drive the stakes in, but I bet it would stay up."

The line was quiet for a few moments.

"Artis, are you there?"

"Yeah."

"Well how about it?"

"This isn't like you."

"Huh?" I never thought about whether my actions were like me or not.

"You never care much about anything either way."

"Yeah I do." But he was right, I didn't.

"All you talk about is this tent. You never talk about anything else. And you want to pitch it in your living room."

"Correct."

"It's sacrilege, Tamar, that's what it is. It's a piece of camping equipment. You use it outside, you know." Artis's voice was thick with scorn.

I began to get angry. Who was he to tell me where I could and couldn't set up my tent? "Well," I said, "I'm starting at two today. If you want to help, come on over. Otherwise, never mind, I'll do it myself."

I placed the receiver in its cradle carefully, evidence, I thought, that nothing bothered me, not even my skeptical Artis. In the kitchen I steeped a cup of tea, resting my face next to the rim so I could feel the steam rising up.

Artis showed up as I was fitting together the eight-foot rod that acts as a beam across the top of the tent.

"Hi. You're late," I said, trying to look engrossed in the instruction booklet.

"Sorry." Artis shook out his umbrella, dropped it on the floor.

"I'm putting in the roof."

"Looks good."

"What's wrong?" I said. Usually Artis talked a mile a minute, telling me the things he had seen on the way over, a new philosophy he had acquired since we last saw each other.

"Nothing." He ran his fingers through his hair, shook the water droplets off his hand. He sat down on the couch and leaned back, slumping into himself. "So, what do you want me to do?"

"I'm almost done here. Doesn't it look beautiful? There's so much blue—it's the perfect size."

Artis nodded.

"In a minute we can crawl in and see how it looks from the in-

146

side." I couldn't wait to zip myself in, to be surrounded by the blue walls and ceiling, my house within a house.

I attached the rod to the shorter metal poles that held up the sides. Now the tent began to have shape, to look like the one on stage the day of the auction, its sides sloping slightly outward from the top. "Boy, am I glad I bought this," I said.

"Yeah, you sure seem to be."

"What do you mean? Of course I'm glad." For a moment I had forgotten Artis was there. His face was red, maybe from the wind outside, maybe because he was upset. I should have paid more attention. Always, I should pay more attention.

"You care more about that damn tent than you ever have for me."

"What?"

Artis clapped his hand over his mouth, as if he couldn't believe his words.

Ridiculous, I thought, this is ridiculous. I'm going out with a man who envies a tent. Artis hunched down, examining the floor, his arms crossed and his elbows on his knees.

"You're jealous. You, a grown man, are jealous of my tent. Is that what you're saying?"

"No. Mostly it's a comment on the way you treat me." Artis sighed. "Do you realize you've never even told me you love me? I tell you all the time. You know what you do?"

I shook my head. Artis always appeared so self-absorbed—it was one reason we'd stayed together: no matter what I did, he always talked, filled up the nooks and crannies, the gaps in our affair.

"You look away. You look at anything besides me. You say the most noncommittal thing, 'Um-hmm,' as if you're not even listening." He stamped his foot on the carpet. "And you play solitaire every night when you know I'm waiting for you to come to bed."

Solitaire—at least I could respond to this. "Artis, I've told you over and over, that's how I think. It helps me find my ideas. You know how it is to work all day and lose your brain."

"Yeah, right. If you don't like sleeping with me, and it's already clear you don't love me, at least take the time to say something."

"Oh, Artis." What could I say? I did like sleeping with him, but I didn't love him. I folded and unfolded the navy blue rain fly. It made a small rustling sound.

"Would you quit that?"

"Sorry. I'm really sorry," I said. I put the fly down.

Artis sat picking at threads on the couch cushion; he wouldn't look me in the eye. He pulled out burgandy-colored bits of string and wound them around his index finger.

"You want to crawl in the tent, see how it looks?" I asked.

"No. No, I don't." He held up his index finger in front of his face, scrutinizing the tip, which had turned an angry purple. "Actually, I think I better leave."

"Okay," I said. I got up to walk him to the door. He pulled his jacket on and buttoned it to his chin. For a moment he looked very small.

"Well, see you," he said, his voice distant.

"Bye," I said. "Sorry about it." I shut the door, turned to survey the room: the tent, the instruction booklet, the stakes and cords strewn across the brown carpet, a plate with a half-eaten sandwich on it, yesterday's newspaper. I told myself, This isn't a sudden thing, certainly not, it's been brewing for months and I just didn't notice. It isn't sudden at all. It happens again and again.

Artis dropped by the other day to pick up his green sweater. He'd left it at my house weeks ago. We couldn't find it for a long time. It was under the bed, covered with dust.

"You should really clean out under there," he said, his voice so nonchalant it seemed stern.

"Why bother? No one ever looks there. Really, I don't know why I should," I said, suddenly contrary.

He nodded. "It's your place."

"Yes, it is."

I could see the vein in Artis's forehead throbbing; he was trying hard to stay calm.

"You still have your tent up, I see," he said, pointing to the tent, sagging slightly in the living room.

"I'm planning to set it up outside sometime soon, maybe in the backyard when it gets a little warmer." I had slept in it the night before, and I hoped he wouldn't peer past the flap to see my pillow and blanket. That morning, the first thing I had seen when I woke was the sloping blue of the tent ceiling, luminescent from the sun shining in the living room window.

"Ah," Artis said, "good."

As he left I patted his shoulder. He leaned a little against me for a moment and was gone, green sweater in hand, all his belongings safely out of my dusty house.

Playing solitaire, I think about how I have always been: what went wrong, how I came to be the way I am today, the point at which it all began. Of course there is no one point. I lay out the cards. Three eights show themselves immediately, and I know I will lose the round. The queen of clubs stares enigmatically up at me, her face somber, a dimple in her chin. Well, she seems to say, and what of it?

I consider the past. In high school I thought I would be someone important one day. It would just happen. I never saw myself doing any specific thing to earn this sense that I mattered, that people would feel glad to be near me.

"You just lost it all," my mother said to me when she heard we were breaking up. "Lost, you've lost it."

I threw up my hands, raised them at the wrists but kept my arms down, a minute gesture. "It doesn't matter."

"What do you mean? Artis was perfect. He could have been it." My mother had plans for us. She, more than anyone, I think, mourns my choice of a tent over a future husband.

"He wasn't it. Nothing's ever it, Mom. My life just goes and goes, that's all, just goes like that, and it's not great and it isn't horrible either."

"You've got to learn to compromise."

"I compromise in my averageness," I said.

My mother shook her head, her white hair brushed forward, her thin lips pursed. She ran her hand across the couch, smoothing it as if it were an animal she had to unruffle.

"I should have known when you were born," she said. "I should have been able to tell, the way you waited and waited to come out, leaving me in labor for hours."

"Oh, come off it," I said. She loved this story, told it to all her friends, the trials of pregnancy.

"Indecisive, even then. Middle-of-the-road, even then." She used the prophetic voice she sometimes musters: You'll see, you'll have regrets. She resembles those people who predict the end of the world within the next week, who warn the uninformed that now is the time to wish for a different past. Perhaps I will have regrets, but I doubt it.

I threw down a paper fan I had been fiddling with. "Well, I'm decisive now. And I know I don't want to marry Artis. I know I don't love him. Okay? You see? You satisfied?"

My mother sat up straight, pulling her hands into her lap, folding them properly. At least she would sit nicely, a response to me, sprawled in an easy chair. "That's not what—" But she didn't finish.

"That's never what you mean," I muttered. "It never is."

I think of my mother, the way I will please her in what she calls my failure, and I wonder who the mother in my dream last night was. Enough, she told me, you have seen enough. These past few weeks, I look forward to the nights in my tent, the way my shadow grows and shrinks with the flashlight, the animal shadows I make with my hands on the walls—rabbits and elongated dogs, toothless wide-jawed alligators—the rustling of my blankets against the tent floor. In the dark it is just me and the blue of the tent and the flashlight. I cannot hear the kitchen faucet dripping. I cannot hear anything outside the tent. I sleep deeply, I sleep well.